'You re_____ured?'
he said.

His eyes held hers. 'Of course you do.' There was a flash of something like respect in his steady gaze.

It was surprisingly difficult to break the eye contact until Jennifer found a way to change the subject. 'What about you?' Fresh drops glistened on the dark grey rock at their feet. 'If you keep bleeding like that *I'll* be the one who has to deal with it.'

Silly, pointless tears were threatening to clog her throat. They were lost on a mountaintop and nobody had any idea where they were. They were all injured to varying degrees and a sub-zero night was about to enfold them.

'Tell you what. I'll splint your arm and you can bandage up my leg.' Guy's forefinger touched Jennifer under her chin and she was startled into raising her face to meet his gaze again. 'We'll look after each other,' he continued softly, 'and that way we'll all get through this. OK?'

'OK.' For an instant, Jennifer really believed that everything *would* be all right. Together, they *would* survive.

A&E DRAMA

Blood pressure is high and pulses are racing in these
fast-paced dramatic stories from Mills & Boon®
Medical Romance™. They'll move a mountain
to save a life in an emergency, be they the crash team,
emergency doctors, or paramedics. There are lots of
critical engagements amongst the high tensions
and emotional passions in these exciting stories
of lives and loves at risk!

HER EMERGENCY KNIGHT

BY
ALISON ROBERTS

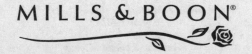

For Sue—a woman of the mountains.
With thanks for your help with the research
and lots of love

First published in Great Britain 2005
Harlequin Mills & Boon Limited,
Eton House, 18-24 Paradise Road, Richmond, Surrey TW9 1SR

© Alison Roberts 2005

ISBN 0 263 84303 3

Set in Times Roman 10½ on 12 pt.
03-0505-48299

Printed and bound in Spain
by Litografía Rosés, S.A., Barcelona

CHAPTER ONE

'MAYDAY... Mayday...'

'Cessna Bravo Papa Tango... Three zero niner... Engine failure...'

'Mayday... Mayday...'

The pilot sounded way too calm for the emergency to be real, Jennifer Allen decided. Mind you, she probably sounded equally dispassionate when calling for, say, a scalpel, buzz-saw and rib spreaders to crack someone's chest in the ED in a desperate last-ditch effort to save a life.

Failure was virtually inevitable in such a scenario. Maybe a radio message requesting assistance for a light plane about to crash into the side of a mountain was a kind of formality as well. Part of a predetermined protocol. Something you did to demonstrate that you'd done absolutely everything possible when any real hope was lost.

'Mayday... Mayday...'

The scenes were badly disjointed. The budget for this movie must have been incredibly low. A wingtip dipped sharply. A woman screamed. The rocks and scree slopes of the terrain were close enough for her to pick out a single alpine flower in a tussock. A mountain buttercup, the real name of which was a Mount Cook lily. That was a nice touch, Jennifer thought, showing the setting to be a New Zealand mountain. Despite only a split-second view, every white petal could be counted, framing the golden centre and looking rather like a floral poached

5

egg. The image was frozen onto her retina by the shock of being suddenly plunged into...nothing.

How had they achieved that total blankness? And why was the theatre so damn cold? Jennifer reached out to pull her bedclothes more securely over her body but she was still too deeply asleep, trapped in the odd dream featuring a disaster movie. She tried to roll over, instead, but the rest of her body was as uncooperative as her arm had been. One foot had gone to sleep and Jennifer could feel the pins and needles of awakening nerves. But wasn't her whole body asleep? The confusing notion made Jennifer want to give up and admire the buttercup again but the image had vanished.

The weight on her body was far more than bedclothes could account for and, strangely, it was steadily increasing. Jennifer didn't have a dog and she had slept alone for years. The weight was now enough to be causing pain—even to make breathing difficult and she made a huge effort to surface from sleep and that lingering dream. To open her eyes and reach out to push the weight away.

Something was terribly wrong.

Jennifer couldn't move. And what she could see only inches from her face had to be an illusion. Part of a dream that wouldn't quit. The hand dangling in mid-air with the fingers an inch or two from the floor was that of a woman. The one that had screamed so piercingly perhaps? The skin texture was that of someone a generation older than herself and the rings that the hand displayed on its fourth finger included a beautiful eternity band of diamonds and sapphires.

The ring seemed oddly familiar and Jennifer could feel herself frowning. The whole hand was familiar, in fact. She had seen it—reaching out for another hand. An older man, with tufty grey hair and a cheeky grin was helping the woman climb into a small plane. Jennifer had already climbed in. She had the tiny back seat of the five-seater plane all to herself and she had been fastening her seat belt and watching the other passengers embark.

'*Mayday… Mayday…*'

The realisation that the 'dream' had been a replay of reality, if not reality itself, hit Jennifer in a single blow. The cold was real. They had been travelling above the bush line over mountainous country. It had been a gloriously sunny spring day, but that was meaningless at an altitude that could collect snow all year round.

The hand was lifeless. Jennifer knew that as instantly as she understood the significance of the ambient temperature. The woman's chest was the object weighing her down and there was not even a flutter of movement that might suggest the woman was still breathing.

Panic clawed at her throat. She had survived a plane crash and now she was trapped beneath a body that probably weighed twice as much as she did. How long ago had they hit the ground? Jennifer had no memory of the impact and she might have only been unconscious for a very short period of time. What had felt like a deep sleep and a drawn-out dream could have been only seconds.

Small planes carried a lot of fuel in their wings. Any moment now and something could ignite and explode.

Jennifer wasn't about to survive a crash landing only to be burned alive, trapped in the tail section of a tiny aircraft, thank you very much. She twisted and pushed, trying to find purchase for her feet.

'*Aah-h!*' Her cry was one of frustration, pain and a not inconsiderable amount of fear.

'Who's that?'

Jennifer's breath caught in a gasp as a mixture of re-lief and hope surged through her. She *wasn't* the only survivor.

'I'm Jennifer Allen,' she called back. She couldn't see anything past the body on top of her. 'Who's that?'

'Guy Knight.'

'Are you the pilot?'

'No.' The tone was slightly dry, suggesting either that being a pilot was not something he would have aspired to—or that Jennifer should have known who he was. Now that she had ruled out the person in charge of the plane, of course, she did know.

Guy Knight was the solid, younger man who had been seated beside the pilot in the front and, yes, she had seen this man before—had heard the name. He'd stood up to ask a quite intelligent question at the end of her presen-tation on managing cardiac tamponade yesterday. But he couldn't really expect her to have remembered the name of one small town or rural GP out of the hundreds who had been attending the weekend conference on emer-gency medicine, could he? They had all seemed to want to talk to her. To ask questions. To pick the brain of one of the conference's keynote speakers.

'I need some help here.' Fear sharpened Jennifer's tone. 'I've got a dead body on top of me and I can't move.'

'Are you injured?''

'I won't be able to tell until I've got out of here. I feel like I've got an elephant sitting on my chest.'

'Shirley always did have a bit of a struggle with her weight.'

A wild desire to point out who was doing the strug-gling now occurred to Jennifer, but the bubble of hys-terical laughter remained trapped, and suffocated as quickly as it had arisen. The reminder that 'the body' was another person was unwelcome. Jennifer needed to focus on her own survival right now. She couldn't afford to be distracted by empathy for any less fortunate people around her. She couldn't help anyone else if she wasn't OK herself, could she?

Dr Guy Knight didn't seem to be in any hurry to live up to his name and offer assistance to a damsel in distress.

'Bill, can you hear me? Bill?'

His voice was close and Jennifer remembered just how small the cabin of this tiny plane was. If a fire started, it would take no time at all for them all to suffocate. Or cook.

'Who the hell is Bill?'

'Shirley's husband. He's a GP in Te Anau. Always loved flying has Bill. He takes any opportunity to get his feet off the ground. I can't get past this… *Damn!*'

Jennifer felt the crushing weight on her chest ease a fraction as she tipped sideways. She also felt the rocks on the other side of the thin metal skin of the fuselage scraping as the tail section of the small plane started sliding. For all Jennifer knew, she was about to go careening down a scree-covered slope and probably into some crevasse, thanks to the idiotic attempts of a wannabe hero to reach someone called Bill.

A tiny part of Jennifer's brain was proud that even such extreme circumstances couldn't push her past the point of self-control into a futile exercise such as screaming in sheer terror. Instead, she swore vehemently and proceeded to let Dr Guy Knight know precisely what she thought of him and his actions that were about to send her plunging to her doom.

'For God's sake,' he snapped at last. 'Will you *shut* up?'

A split second of astonished silence followed the interruption.

'You've moved a whole six inches at the most,' Dr Knight continued. 'The tail is now wedged against a rock that's not going anywhere for another million years or so.'

He was right, Jennifer realised. The terrifying movement had ceased completely. Her heart was still thumping erratically, however, and her breathing was a series of painful gasps. Shutting up was probably very sensible.

Guy Knight wasn't shutting up. He also seemed to be attacking the plane wreckage in some fashion. Jerks and thumps reverberated through the surface Jennifer lay on.

'I've only managed to get Digger out so far and he's not looking too flash right now. You've got two people on top of you and if Bill was conscious he might be able to help me get him out.'

No wonder the weight was so restricting. Jennifer concentrated on her breathing. Slow and deep, she repeated over and over to herself. Hyperventilating wasn't going to help and might already be responsible for the pins and needles now evident in her fingertips as well as her foot.

'But he can't help.' Dr Knight sounded angry now and his tone was underscored by the harsh scrape of metal on rock. 'Because he's dead.'

Dragging sounds could be heard now and Jennifer felt her breathing ease a little more. The unfortunate Bill was clearly being moved out of the way. For *her* benefit. She should be feeling very grateful that someone was making what was probably an enormous effort to rescue her. Instead, an irrational anger generated by the fact that she was unable to help herself blossomed. It was heavily laced with embarrassment at her eloquent attack on the intelligence of the man she was now dependent on for assistance.

A few seconds' silence fell when the dragging ceased. Jennifer heard a faint cough and then a groan from somewhere outside. Maybe Bill was still alive after all, unless the sound had come from the man with a name like some kind of construction machinery. Had it been Dozer? Guy's voice cut through the thought, sounding low and reassuring—nothing like the tone in which he had been speaking to her. Then silence fell again, for long enough to alarm Jennifer.

Why hadn't he come back? *Was* he coming back? Had venting her fear in such an aggressive manner made him decide to leave her where she was until a rescue team arrived? The comforting thought that an emergency locator beacon would have been activated by the crash, and help was probably already on the way, was enough to reassure Jennifer that she wasn't totally dependent on the man moving around outside.

She didn't give a damn what he thought of her or her vocabulary anyway. She could get herself out of here. With the weight of only one person on top of her now, it should be possible to inch her way clear, despite the sardine can of metal embracing her. She certainly wasn't going to beg for help, that was for sure.

Twisting didn't help. Neither did pushing. The limp arm Jennifer managed to shift flopped back, giving a muted thud as the hand hit the metal surface her cheek was pressed against. The gruesome reminder of just how serious this situation was punctured the renewed anger that had fuelled Jennifer's efforts to extricate herself. The energising emotion dissipated, leaving a physical exhaustion that allowed fear a new foothold.

Her arm hurt. A lot. And it was still too hard to catch a deep enough breath. For one horrible moment Jennifer thought she was going to give up and burst into tears of despair.

'You still OK in there?'

He had come back. Jennifer pressed her lips together and squeezed her eyes tightly shut, using sheer will-power to strangle the weakness tears would have betrayed.

'Hey...Dr Allen? Talk to me.'

So he *did* care whether she was still alive. The concern in the voice was almost her undoing and Jennifer couldn't trust herself to answer without giving in to a sob...or pleading for help.

'Jennifer? Can you hear me? Are you all right?'

'I will be.' Jennifer pushed each word out carefully, still fighting for control. 'When I get the hell out of here. Are you going to *help* me or not?'

'Right away, ma'am.' The tone was dry enough to stop just short of sarcasm. 'I've just got to get Shirley's legs out from under what's left of this door.'

It seemed to take far too long. The wreckage rocked and Jennifer heard grunts of exertion and the occasional oath, followed by loud hammering as though a rock was being used on a piece of uncooperative metal. And then, finally, the weight was being removed, inch by inch. Jennifer found she could turn onto her back and use one arm, then her legs, to help push the burden clear.

She twisted back onto her stomach to wriggle clear of her prison but froze as she felt a large, firm hand on her leg. Her thigh, of all places, on *bare* skin—well above the level that her skirt should have covered.

'Watch out! There's a sharp edge of metal right here. I can't bend it back any more. I've already tried.'

Jennifer moved her leg away from the hand but it wasn't letting go.

'*Stop!*' There was a rough edge to Guy's voice that made obedience unquestionable.

'What *now?*' If Shirley's body had fitted through the gap, there must be more than enough room for Jennifer to follow safely.

'There's a first-aid kit that should be in there somewhere. It was kept underneath your seat.'

'I didn't see it.'

'It's red. Looks like a large flat sports bag.'

Jennifer *could* see something red, close to where her head had been resting in the pocket behind the original position of her seat. She would have to crawl downhill to reach it now, and interrupting her path to freedom was the last thing she wanted to do.

'We're going to need it.' Guy's tone was firm. 'And I'm not sure I can fit in there.'

After a long moment's hesitation Jennifer gritted her teeth and forced herself to inch back. She hooked her fingers into the piece of synthetic red fabric showing and pulled. A wave of pain sharp enough to make her head spin shot up her arm. The sensation inside her arm was unmistakable. A broken bone had just moved, scraping against another piece of bone in the process.

Jennifer flexed her fingers. At least she wasn't showing any signs of neurological compromise. It might be her left hand but she still needed it to function perfectly in the job she did. Her right hand felt fine so she used just that one to pull at the bag again.

A query floated in from behind. 'What's taking so long?'

'It's stuck,' Jennifer said shortly. 'I can't get it out.'

'Try harder.'

'I'm doing my best, dammit!' Nobody had ever had to tell Jennifer to try harder. Anger resurfaced and Jennifer took hold of the bag with both hands again. She was angry enough not to care how much it hurt and maybe if she pulled in a straight line she could exert enough pressure without passing out from pain. The subsequent tug was enough to move the bag several inches from where it was wedged beneath torn leather upholstery and broken springs. 'OK...I think I've got it!'

'Good girl!'

Good *girl?* That kind of approval hadn't been bestowed on her since she was a child. Jennifer Allen was thirty-four years old now and sought respect from others, not a pat on the head. So why did she feel so ridiculously proud of this achievement? And so determined to keep hold of the awkward red bag and complete its delivery? Pulling in a straight line seemed to be working. The pain was still sharp but there was no sickening crunch of bones that would provoke a vagal reaction.

The question of why she felt so proud of herself was still unanswerable by the time she reached the verge of freedom, but at least it provided a distraction from the feel of Guy Knight's hands as they held her legs, then her hips, as she wriggled past a mangled door and shredded metal to find herself standing on solid ground.

Well, almost standing. Her legs felt like jelly and the light was bright enough to make her eyes water furiously so Jennifer kept them tightly closed. She clutched the red bag to her chest and didn't protest as she felt herself being eased into a sitting position.

'Were you knocked out?' Strong fingers were palpating her head and neck.

'I must have been, I guess. I remember waking up.'

'Can you remember what day it is?'

'Sunday. And it must be around 5:00 p.m.' Jennifer was quite confident that her level of consciousness was not impaired despite her mild headache. 'We got on the plane at four o'clock and that pilot reckoned it would take over an hour to get anywhere near Fox Glacier.'

'It's just after 5:00 p.m. now. Are you having any trouble breathing?'

'Not anymore.'

'Can you open your eyes?'

Jennifer complied, blinking and squinting as she tried to adjust to the glare of sunlight. The GP's face was very close to her own. Dark eyes fringed with long, black lashes were assessing her from beneath a flop of equally dark hair. A minor laceration on his temple had stopped bleeding but had left a smear of blood now mixed with grime over rather angular features. A strong face, Jennifer thought distractedly. And not a particularly friendly one.

'Does anything hurt?'

Jennifer felt as though she'd been run over by a train. Things ached and stung in all sorts of places but no single pain stood out as being unbearable. Even the arm she knew she had broken was just a dull throb now that she'd stopped putting stress on it. The man in front of her looked in worse shape. A nasty abrasion covered the side of one arm and bloodstains covered large areas of his white shirt and faded denim jeans.

'I'm OK.' Jennifer was still staring at Guy Knight's legs. 'Whose blood is that?'

'Probably Bill's.' Guy didn't bother to look down. He gave a brief nod instead. 'You look OK.' A hand reached out. 'I'll take that bag, then. Digger needs some help.'

Jennifer released the bag she'd forgotten she was clutching. 'Who's Digger?'

'The pilot.'

'Oh.'

'This *wasn't* his fault.' The swift reaction to any implied criticism in Jennifer's tone was sharp. 'If Digger
hadn't coped with that engine failure as well as he did,
we'd all be dead.' Turning abruptly, Dr Knight walked
away.

Jennifer pushed herself to her feet, pleased to find her
legs working far more normally. She was standing in the
space between a wing that had broken completely free
and the bulk of the Cessna. The propeller blades of the
single engine were crumpled almost beyond recognition
and the front window and part of the plane's roof had
been torn away.

Lettering on the other end of the fuselage was dis-
torted. B... P... L. No. An echo of Jennifer's dream
sounded in her head. That last letter was a T.

'Bravo Papa Tango... Mayday... Mayday...'

Jennifer's gaze slid involuntarily to her fellow passengers now lying beside the wreckage. She should check
that they were, indeed, beyond any help a doctor could
provide, but she didn't move. Nobody could survive the
kind of head injury Bill had clearly sustained and she
had been in close enough contact with Shirley for long
enough to know that she, also, was dead. Taking the time
to confirm what she already knew was pointless. Turning
her back on the fatalities, Jennifer picked her way over
rocks and tussocks, following her new companion to
where the sharply bent, sheared-off wing had created a
kind of wall. The man with tufty grey hair lay behind
the wing tip. Guy was standing beside him.

'Digger? Can you hear me, mate?'

The response was incoherent and Jennifer's view of
the other survivor was blocked as Guy crouched in front

of her. It was tempting to focus on the injured man herself but Jennifer needed a moment or two to orient herself first. This was no well-equipped emergency department with extra staff and facilities available automatically.

How ironic, to find herself in a situation like this, having travelled the length of the country to give GPs her expert advice on how to handle emergencies in precisely such situations. Now she was about to find out, at first-hand, what it was like to depend on limited resources and personal skills. Already she was listening for the sound of an engine. A buzz that would evolve into the chop of rotors as a rescue helicopter arrived to break the barrier of isolation.

No sound broke the overwhelming silence around them, however, and Jennifer's gaze was drawn as involuntarily towards the horizon as it had been to the bodies beside the plane. She knew she would see a reality she would rather not confront. She also knew that it had to *be* confronted before she could move on. Scanning the clear blue of the sky in the hope of seeing a sign of movement offered no reassurance, but what she did see took her breath away.

Alongside and above for as far as she could see were the sharp peaks and valleys of the Southern Alps—a mountain range that provided a spine for the south island of New Zealand. Sunlight turned patches of snow into the blinding glare of mirrors and shadowed surrounding grey rock into inky darkness. Barren heights became the kind of tussock-covered terrain she was stranded on at present and bush-covered slopes fanned out below, a thick, green blanket softening variations in the terrain that were probably as sharp as those created by the towering peaks.

Jennifer had grown up in this country. New Zealand was home and it had always offered the security of being small and relatively isolated from the evils the rest of the world had to endure, but there was nothing remotely small about this landscape. The vast emptiness made her feel astonishingly insignificant.

No wonder people—and planes—got lost out here, never to be recovered. Even with a beacon sending out a distress call, Jennifer had no idea how long it might take for their exact location to be pinpointed. Maybe you had to fly within range to pick it up in the first place, and there were thousands of square miles to cover out there.

She was alone.

No. *They* were alone.

Jennifer swallowed past the constriction in her throat as she dragged her gaze back to the crouching man in front of her. She found herself the object of a speculative glance.

'If you've finished admiring the view,' Guy Knight said mildly, 'I could use some help here.'

CHAPTER TWO

ANSWERING a call to duty was automatic.

Absorbing the reality of what had happened and where they were had taken only seconds, but the effect was an anchorage from which Jennifer could now function without distraction. Locking into the practice of what she was most competent to perform was a relief. A way of taking back control in the midst of catastrophe.

'Airway?'

'Clear.' Guy Knight was opening the red sports bag. Jennifer could see neatly rolled packages and caught a glimpse of cardboard splints lining the base of the bag as some items were pulled clear. She should take the time to use one to splint her forearm, but it didn't actually hurt too badly anymore and she could wriggle her fingers and even make a fist without causing more than fairly tolerable discomfort. It was a minor injury compared to what the man on the ground had suffered and, as such, it could wait.

'Has he been conscious at all?' Jennifer stepped around Guy's feet to get to the other side of their patient. The two-inch heel of her shoe caught between two rocks but she ignored the discomfort the lurching movement provoked. She had obviously collected quite a few sprains and bruises, but hopefully the only broken bone was in her arm. 'What's his name?'

'He was alert enough to get out of the plane by himself. He was obviously short of breath and said his ribs hurt, but it took a bit of convincing to get him to sit down while I went back to see about the rest of you. It wasn't until I'd got Bill out and went back to check that I found him less responsive.'

He'd still gone back to help Jennifer out of the wreckage, however. She owed both these men the best she had to offer right now.

'Name?'

'Jim Spade. But he hasn't willingly answered to anything other than "Digger" for as long as I've known him.'

Jennifer leaned close and rubbed a knuckle on the older man's sternum. 'Digger! Can you hear me? Open your eyes.'

The man groaned and his eyes opened briefly. He jerked his head and his hands moved, but any struggle to speak was clearly too much of an effort.

'Breathing's inadequate,' Jennifer stated. 'Do you carry an oxygen cylinder in that bag?'

'No.'

'Bag mask?'

'No.'

'Stethoscope?'

'Yes.'

'Good.' Jennifer's tone implied that he had, at last, provided an acceptable answer. She took the item from Guy's hands and flicked off the leather jacket draped over Digger's chest. It was only then that she realised why Guy seemed so inappropriately clothed for the cold temperature. He had been wearing this jacket over his polo-type shirt when he had boarded the small plane.

Digger had a woollen plaid bush shirt on, the buttons of which only opened a short distance.

'Got some shears?' Jennifer queried.

'Don't think so.'

'We need this shirt off. I can't see what's going on.'

Guy leaned forward. He gripped the shirt at the base of the neck opening and ripped the heavy fabric apart as easily as if it had been a light cotton.

'Sorry, Digger. It's about time you treated yourself to a new one anyway.'

The T-shirt beneath was ripped from the hem upwards and they both stared at the exposed, skinny chest for a moment as they assessed the chest-wall movement. Breathing was rapid and shallow. Then Guy pointed.

'Look at that.'

'Mmm.' Jennifer gave no sign of being impressed at such rapid recognition of a life-threatening situation. 'Paradoxical chest-wall motion.'

As Digger breathed in and his chest wall moved outward, an area on the left side sank inwards. With an inward breath, it bulged outwards. The movement was subtle because of the shallow respirations but that did nothing to diminish its significance. Several ribs had been broken in two or more places, resulting in a section floating free that would seriously compromise breathing.

Jennifer's hand had gone straight to the area and she elicited a heavy groan from Digger as she stabilised the flail segment in an inward position.

'We need some towels, or sandbags, or a pillow. And a wide bandage.' Jennifer looked up to catch Guy's raised eyebrow and an almost patient expression on his face. OK, so she wasn't in her emergency department or even the back of a well-equipped ambulance. She could cope.

'We'll just use his arm as a splint, then. You *do* have some bandages, don't you?'

Having the arm bound to the chest wall to keep the floating ribs in place made the rest of the assessment of

Digger's breathing more awkward, but his respiratory distress seemed to be easing slowly. A faint pink tinge crept back into his skin and his level of consciousness was improving. Opening his eyes, Digger tried to cough but the attempt was weak and broken by an agonised groan.

'Let's position him on his injured side,' Jennifer directed, lifting the stethoscope from Digger's chest. 'He's moving air but breath sounds are definitely reduced on the left side. We want to keep his uninjured lung functioning as well as possible.' She sighed. 'I wish we had some oxygen. Or at least a bag mask.'

'Welcome to the world of front-line emergency care,' Guy responded. He gently eased an arm beneath the older man as he spoke, tilting him single-handedly towards his left side. Digger groaned again. 'Sorry, mate,' Guy said. 'We're just trying to look after you. We'll get something for that pain as soon as we can.'

'You've got morphine?' Jennifer was pleasantly surprised.

'Only a few ampoules, but it should help for a while.'

'Should be more than enough.' Jennifer nodded. 'How long will it take for a rescue helicopter to get to us?'

She didn't wait for a response. Her patient's airway and breathing were under as much control as they could achieve for the moment, and she wanted an assessment of his circulation. Picking up Digger's wrist, Jennifer felt for a radial pulse. Frowning, she shifted her grip and tried again.

'Barely palpable,' she announced. 'Have you got a BP cuff in that kit?'

'No. We don't have a defibrillator or a 12-lead ECG either.' Guy was pulling his fleece-lined leather jacket back over Digger's chest. 'I'm afraid you'll have to make do with good old-fashioned estimates. If the radial pulse is palpable, his systolic is at least 80, which is adequate for renal perfusion.'

'Hardly adequate to administer morphine,' Jennifer countered sharply. 'And it wasn't an unreasonable request. Sphygmomanometers hardly cost the earth these days, and many are quite small enough for any first-aid kit. I would have thought you'd use one often enough to make it an essential item even in a remote practice.'

'*My* first-aid kit happens to be in the back of my four-wheel-drive vehicle and it's perfectly well equipped, thank you. I keep one in Digger's plane as backup simply because I often fly with him. The morphine's not exactly legal with it not being under lock and key, but we needed it once and didn't have it so we bent the rules.'

'Oh.' Jennifer didn't bother to apologise for the incorrect assumption regarding Guy's medical practice. 'He's a friend of yours, then?'

The smile was fleeting enough to be no more than a ghost. 'You could say that.'

'Has he got any medical conditions I should know about?' Jennifer was running her hands over Digger's body in a sweep for any obvious bleeding. 'How old is he?'

'Seventy-two.'

'And he's still *flying?*'

'Any reason why he shouldn't be?'

Jennifer met the angry stare without flinching. Only the obvious, she wanted to say. This flight hadn't exactly been a huge success, had it? The steely glare from those dark eyes silenced her, however. If the pilot had any major physical problems like a cardiac condition, the civil aviation authority wouldn't have renewed his licence. Assuming that Digger *was* still licensed, of course, but Jennifer wasn't about to go there.

'Any allergies that you know of?'

'No. He had a hip replacement about ten years ago but he's as fit as a fiddle otherwise. Not that he'd tell me in a hurry if he wasn't.' Guy was smiling down at the man lying between them. 'He's as tough as an old boot is Digger. He's probably broken every bone in his body at least once, thanks to his early days as a rodeo rider. He cut his leg badly with a chainsaw once and sewed himself up with dental floss before driving fifty miles to come and find me.'

Jennifer's grunt indicated either a lack of interest in anecdotes or concentration on her current task of palpating Digger's abdomen. When she got to the upper left quadrant, Digger groaned and opened his eyes.

'Hurts…'

'OK, I'll stop pushing.' Jennifer was pleased to see her patient looking more alert. 'You've had a nasty knock on your left side. You've got broken ribs and may have some internal injuries. How does your breathing feel now?'

'Bit…better…'

'You need some fluids,' Jennifer told him. 'Dr Knight here is going to put a needle in your hand now.' She glanced up swiftly, having heard what sounded like a faintly incredulous snort. 'Is that a problem?' she asked evenly. 'You have fluids in that kit. I was assuming you also had the IV gear to make use of them.'

'Oh, I do,' Guy responded.

'Then what's the problem?'

'No problem.' Guy clearly wasn't going to be the first to break eye contact. 'It was just your other assumption that I found kind of amusing.' An eyebrow rose. 'You're used to being in charge, aren't you, Dr Allen?'

Jennifer felt muscles in her jaw tighten as she watched Guy pull a tie on a package from the kit, unrolling it to reveal a good supply of cannulae, swabs, luer plugs and occlusive dressings. He had asked for her help, hadn't he? As the most highly qualified person present, of course she had assumed command of the scene.

'And you must be used to being a big fish in a little pond.' Her smile lacked any hint of warmth. 'Why don't *I* put the IV line in?'

'Works for me.' Guy's smile was just as chilly as hers had been. 'I'll go and see if I can find what we need to get Digger a bit more comfortable and keep him warm.'

'Try the radio while you're there,' Jennifer instructed. 'I'd like to know how far away rescue is.'

The arm she was encircling with a tourniquet moved as Digger raised his hand.

'Stuffed,' he said succinctly. 'Radio's…shot.'

'I'm sure Dr Knight is responsible enough to carry a cell phone. If he isn't, then mine is in my bag…wherever that is.'

The snort from Guy was unmistakable this time. 'And how many transmitter towers did you spot on the way, *Dr* Allen?'

The sound from Digger could have been a groan. Or a growl.

'Cut it…out,' he said clearly. 'You're behaving…like children.' Despite having to take short gasps of air every few words, he continued speaking. 'My fault we're here… Going to be a while… Rather not listen to…squabbling.'

Squabbling? She was never that unprofessional, especially when dealing with less qualified subordinates.

And just how long was 'a while'? An hour? Two, maybe? The puff of air around her lower legs as she moved was icy, and Jennifer realised that the chill was why her fingers seemed to be lacking their usual dexterity as she snapped the cap off a cannula.

It was ridiculous to be engaging in some sort of power play with a rural GP who apparently wasn't impressed by her position or personality. Or maybe he was still in a huff because she hadn't recognised him from yesterday's question-and-answer session. None of that mattered a damn right now because none of them were safe yet. Not by a long shot. She bit her lip as she glanced up to see Guy turning back towards the wreckage of the plane.

'If you can find something to prop Digger up with, I'd be grateful,' she called. 'Lying flat isn't going to help his breathing.'

A hand was raised in acknowledgement but Guy didn't turn his head so Jennifer didn't bother to call out any thanks. She turned back to the task at hand.

'Sharp scratch now, Digger.' It took several seconds of careful needle-tip manoeuvring to gain access to a vein flattened by low blood pressure. 'Sorry,' Jennifer murmured. 'I know it hurts.'

'It's nothing,' Digger said. 'And *I'm* the one…who should be sorry, lass.'

'This wasn't your fault,' Jennifer found herself saying. 'And according to Guy, if you hadn't handled things as well as you did then none of us would have made it.'

'Shirley?' Digger's voice was rough. 'And Bill? Are they…?'

Jennifer shook her head, meeting his gaze only briefly before reaching for the luer plug to cap the end of the cannula.

'Oh…*God!*' Digger squeezed his eyes shut. By the time he opened them again, Jennifer had taped the IV into place and attached the giving set. She held the bag of saline aloft and opened the flow.

'What did you say…your name was?'

'Actually, I didn't say.' Jennifer's smile was rueful. 'Rude of me, wasn't it? I'm Jennifer Allen.'

'You're the…big shot…from Auckland, yeah?'

'Yeah.' The smile was matched by a dismissive head-shake. 'Not that that's going to be much help up here.'

'I'll be right.' A faint smile tugged at Digger's lips. 'I've got…nine lives.'

'But how many of them have you used up already?' Guy had returned, carrying what looked like the back of a seat. He also held a bulky, pale blue item of clothing.

'Put this on,' he directed Jennifer. 'The sunlight's not going to be around much longer and it's going to get bloody cold.'

The padded anorak looked inviting but Jennifer hesitated. Guy's face softened almost imperceptibly. 'Shirley doesn't need it anymore,' he said quietly. One corner of his mouth tilted. 'And it should keep you warm—it's big enough to go round you twice. Here, I'll hold that bag while you put it on, then we can get this seat behind Digger.'

The instant warmth was comforting. 'Thanks…Guy.'

'You're welcome…Jennifer.'

So they were to be on an equal footing. Fair enough. 'What about you?' Jennifer's gaze slid to Guy's bare arms. 'Aren't you freezing?'

'I'll go back and get Bill's jacket in a minute. Let's sort Digger out first.'

It wasn't the first time Jennifer had gained the impression that this man was used to putting other people first. She felt a pang of remorse that she hadn't enquired into his welfare before this. That blood on the leg of his jeans still looked remarkably fresh. If it had all come from Bill, why hadn't it congealed and darkened by now? As soon as they made the pilot as comfortable as possible, she would make it her business to check Guy out properly. She'd need to do something about her own arm as well. Doctors really were the worst patients.

'I don't suppose you've got a foil sheet or something in that kit, do you? It would be good to get something between Digger and the ground.'

'Sure.' Guy handed back the bag of IV fluid but Jennifer didn't want to stand and hold it.

'Could you pass me some tape?' She almost sighed at the now familiar look she received. 'Please?'

Threading the tape through the hole at the top of the bag, Jennifer then looped long sticky sections in a figure of eight around the upper edge of the wingtip.

'Bit fat for an IV pole but it'll do the job.'

'Good thinking.' Guy held up two small packages. 'Foil sheets.'

'Great. Let's get sorted, then.'

For the next ten minutes they were both kept busy. They wrapped Digger in the sheets to help prevent the loss of body heat. They used rocks to stabilise the cushioned seat back and got it into a position so that Digger was propped up to assist respiration but still tilted to his injured side. They also tucked him a little more closely into the windbreak provided by the bent wing. Hoping that the fluids were raising blood pressure enough to make it safe to administer some pain relief, Jennifer reached under the cover of the leather jacket to find Digger's wrist.

She found her fingers grasped and saw a reminder of the cheeky grin she had noticed much earlier that day.

'The lengths some people…have to go to…to get a pretty girl…to hold their hand!'

'Hmm.' Jennifer couldn't help grinning. 'You could have just asked! How's the pain?'

'Pretty…bad.'

The grin faded as she turned to Guy. 'Much stronger pulse now. Do you want to draw up some morphine?'

'OK.' Guy's gaze was fixed on Digger and for a split second Jennifer saw a level of concern in his eyes that was far more than a doctor would normally show for a patient. Even a patient who was a friend. There was a bond between these two men that made special care of Digger paramount and Jennifer found herself reaching for the stethoscope. While things appeared to be stable right now, this man had at least two potentially life-threatening injuries.

'How's the chest?' Guy's expression was nothing more than professional now as he drew sterile saline into a syringe to dilute the contents of the morphine ampoule.

'Clear on the right. Still moving air on the left, but I think the breath sounds have diminished since the last time I listened. A pneumothorax is pretty likely, given those rib injuries. We'll just have to keep our fingers crossed that it doesn't tension.'

Their eyes met with only the briefest of looks. Enough to acknowledge just how quickly this scene could turn to custard. Enough to confirm that they would both be doing their best to manage any complications—and to succeed.

A thin stream of fluid sprayed from a needle tip as Guy removed the air bubble from the syringe. 'I thought

I'd do this in five-milligram increments,' he announced. 'If that's all right with you, Dr Allen?'

'Works for me, Dr Knight.'

The formal use of titles was more an agreement to work as equals than the previous form of a putdown, but Digger clearly didn't approve.

'Cut the "Doctor" bit,' he growled. 'Anyone would think…that I was…sick or something.'

The first dose of morphine dulled his pain but not sufficiently to make re-examination of his abdomen a pleasant experience.

'Definite guarding in the left upper quadrant,' Jennifer informed Guy.

'Talk English,' Digger growled.

'You've got a sore gut,' Guy told him.

'Could have…told *you* that, son… What's…broken, then?'

'You might have dented your spleen. Possibly a bit of your liver. They could be cut and bleeding a bit.'

Jennifer eyed the bag of IV fluid. One litre was almost gone and they only had two more. If Digger did have an abdominal bleed from a laceration to either his spleen or liver, they would be in trouble before very long. She pulled the remnants of Digger's woollen shirt back to cover him before tucking the leather jacket in place.

'Thanks…Jenna.'

Jennifer's gaze lifted sharply. 'Why did you call me that?'

'Don't like…Jennifer. Too posh.'

The approving smirk on Guy's face was hardly subtle. Jennifer just stared as he leaned towards the older man.

'How's your pain now, Digger?'

'Bit better.'

'On a scale of one to ten?'

'Twelve.'

'What was it before that dose of jungle juice?'

'Twenty-five.'

'Right.' Guy shook his head. 'Never one to conform, are you?'

'Nope.'

'And maybe Jennifer *likes* her posh name.'

She wasn't going to stay silent while they reinforced their branding of her as some sort of outsider.

'It's not *posh,*' she informed them loftily. 'Neither am I.'

Guy's snort of amusement was outrageous.

'What—' Jennifer demanded, 'is *that* supposed to mean?'

'Well, come on! You're the epitome of "posh,"' Guy shot back. 'Nice hair, nice clothes, great education. Top job in one of the country's leading hospitals. Good grief, you even chose to wear high heels and a suit to go out sightseeing.'

'This isn't a suit! Just a skirt and top…and jacket.'

'Looks like a matching set to me. They'd be getting the lace doilies out in the Glenfalloch pub if you showed up looking like that.'

'I have no intention of setting foot in the Glenfalloch pub—wherever that may be.'

'It's my local,' Guy said casually. 'The best pub in Central and about the only building of any note between where I live and Wanaka.'

'It's my local…too.' Digger sounded drowsy. 'I'd give my left arm for a…pint or two…right now.' He opened his eyes enough to give Jennifer an appraising glance. 'You're right, though, son…she's a looker… Reminds me…of Diana.'

'I was referring to the image of a city slicker,' Guy said. 'Not dishing out compliments.'

'Cheers,' Jennifer murmured.

'Not that you don't deserve a compliment, of course.' Guy finished injecting the second dose of morphine. 'I just wouldn't want you to think I was hitting on you.'

'Perish the thought,' Jennifer agreed drily.

She shook her head. What a bizarre conversation to be having, given the circumstances. Or perhaps it wasn't. The three of them had been hurled into dealing with an appalling situation together. The more of a bond they could form, the more they could help each other survive. Already Jennifer felt very differently towards Digger than she would have if he'd been lying on a bed in her emergency department. And for a few seconds there she had actually forgotten they were crouched on a mountaintop with a tangle of crushed metal and two dead bodies nearby.

'I don't mind being called Jenna,' she told Digger somewhat hesitantly. 'It's just that the only person who ever did was my dad and…' Her voice was annoyingly wobbly. 'And it just startled me a bit, I guess. My dad died not so long ago.' She cleared her throat. 'It's time we hung a new bag of fluid, Guy. No.' She scrambled to her feet. 'I'll get it. You need to go and find that jacket. You're turning blue.'

'OK. I'll see what else I can salvage at the same time.'

'Try the…side hatch.' Digger had his eyes closed again but was looking a lot more comfortable. 'There's a few…camping supplies.'

Moving seemed to have the effect of lowering the temperature sharply. Body warmth was quickly lost as the surrounding chill seeped under the folds of Jennifer's skirt and sneaked down the back of her neck. Her toes

felt numb and her fingers fumbled as they tried to remove the tab protecting the port of the saline pouch and
insert the spike of the giving set. She stopped for a moment to blow on her hands and rub them together.

Looking past the edge of the wingtip as she taped the
new bag into place, Jennifer could see Guy picking his
way around the tail of the plane wreckage some distance
away. The bent wing that had snapped off the Cessna
and was now sheltering Digger had left a gap that the
small plane seemed to have folded itself into. Was that
why those sitting in the middle had fared so much worse
than the others?

The hollow tail section that Jennifer had been wedged
into was angled down to where the rudder was lodged
between two huge rocks. Guy was using a much smaller
rock to hammer at a flap that must be some kind of
luggage compartment. Jennifer was pleased to see he
was now wearing a dark blue padded jacket, similar in
style to her paler version.

The light was changing by the time Guy returned. The
sun was lower and faint wisps of cloud and snow pockets
on distant peaks were tinged faintly pink.

'I found a tarp,' Guy said with satisfaction. 'And a
billy. I even found some food. The dried soup won't be
much use without hot water, but there's a packet of
chocolate biscuits.'

'Never know when you...might need a Tim Tam,'
Digger murmured.

'I'm going to collect some rocks,' Guy told Jennifer.
'We'll use the wingtip as a support and anchor the tarp.
If we can keep the three of us sheltered as close together
as possible, we should get through the night OK.'

'The *night?*' Jennifer didn't care that the word came

out as a frightened squeak. 'They'll come before then, won't they?'

Guy moved a hand towards the orange glow beginning to silhouette the mountains. 'We've got about thirty minutes of useful daylight left. If they had any idea where we are, they would have flown at least close enough for us to see them by now.'

'There is an emergency locator beacon on board, isn't there?' The way both men avoided her gaze was unnerving. '*Isn't* there?'

Digger mumbled something about it all being his fault and then closed his eyes as though his pain level was again intolerable. Guy jerked his head.

'Come and help me with these rocks.'

Jennifer followed him until they were out of Digger's earshot. 'Are you going to tell me what that was all about?' she demanded.

'They've been waiting for some new beacons to come in. About a month ago there was an incident that showed a certain batch of beacons to be faulty. A batch that included the one on this plane. They ordered the new ones straight away, of course, but so did everyone else. There was a waiting list.'

'So...' Jennifer's tongue found a tiny laceration on the inside of her cheek as she absorbed the information. 'What you're saying is that the beacon on our plane may not have been activated at all. They might not even be looking for us.'

'Oh, they'll be looking.'

'But?'

Guy sighed heavily as he reached down to pick up a rock. 'But probably not around here.'

'Why not?'

'Sightseeing flights normally take in the lakes and the fiords. A round trip down to Milford Sound and back.'

'So?'

'So we went the other way. To find the glaciers.'

Jennifer picked up a rock and tucked it into the crook of her left elbow, making her arm ache with renewed strength. She ignored the pain. 'Digger must have filed a flight plan.'

'He did.'

'Good.'

'No. His plan was for the Milford run.'

'So why the hell did he change direction?'

Guy had three rocks in his arms now. 'Because someone important wanted to see the bloody glaciers, that's why.'

'This isn't *my* fault!' Jennifer glared at Guy but he was busy searching for rather scarce stones of a manageable weight. 'He asked me what I wanted to see. How was I supposed to know? Nobody disagreed. Including *you*.' Jennifer swooped on another rock but her arm protested viciously at the extra weight and both rocks fell to the ground. 'Oh, *dammit!*'

Guy caught at her upper arm, his own rocks abandoned, as Jennifer reached down again. 'Let me see that arm.'

'It's fine.'

'Like hell it is.' Guy's fingers were on the now swollen flesh, having pushed up the sleeves of her anorak, jacket and soft jumper. His touch was gentle but firm and there was no way Jennifer could suppress her flinch as the ends of her broken bone moved against each other.

Guy caught her gaze. 'You realise this is fractured?' His eyes held hers. 'Of course you do.' There was a flash of something like respect in his steady gaze. 'Were you going to do something about it or just carry on collecting rocks?'

'We need the rocks.' It was surprisingly difficult to break the eye contact, but the rocks in question provided a new focus until Jennifer found a way to change the subject. 'What about you? That's *not* Bill's blood, is it?'

Fresh drops glistened on the dark grey rock at their feet. 'We don't have enough fluid for two people in shock,' Jennifer reminded him. 'And if you keep bleeding like that, *I'll* be the one who has to deal with it.'

Her tone sharpened as she spoke. Silly, pointless tears were threatening to clog her throat. They were lost on a mountaintop and nobody had any idea where they were. They were all injured to varying degrees and a sub-zero night was about to enfold them.

'Tell you what. We'll get the tarp in place and then I'll splint your arm and you can bandage up my leg.' Guy's forefinger touched Jennifer under her chin and she was startled into raising her face to meet his gaze again. 'We'll look after each other,' he continued softly, 'and that way, we'll all get through this. OK?'

'OK.' For an instant, Jennifer really believed that everything *would* be all right. Together, they *would* survive. Guy's strength was obvious, both emotionally from the reassurance he was able to impart and physically, which he demonstrated by picking up his own collection of brick-sized rocks and then the two Jennifer had found.

His gentleness became apparent a little later as he bound Jennifer's forearm to a small cardboard splint, and his stamina was evident when he unflinchingly tolerated her ministrations to a badly grazed arm, a deeply lacerated calf and possibly a fractured ankle that had swollen far more than her arm had.

By the time they had finished their first aid on each

other and had crawled inside the shelter they had created around Digger, a darkness more complete than Jennifer had ever experienced enfolded them. They checked their patient by the light of the torch Guy had had in his kit and then settled, one of either side of Digger, to help keep him warm.

'Nice,' Digger murmured. 'If I just asked…would you hold my hand…again, Jenna?'

A few seconds later Jennifer heard loud crackling noises coming from Guy's side.

'Hey, Jenna?'

'Yeah?'

'Could I interest you in a Tim Tam?'

The bubble of laughter took Jennifer completely by surprise. Here she was, crowded into a makeshift low tent with two men who had been strangers to her only hours previously. They were facing what was probably going to be the longest night of their lives, but the danger they faced had somehow bonded them into a unit that felt more like a family than Jennifer had felt part of for many, many years.

A chocolate biscuit should be well down on any wish list right now. A helicopter would have been at the top of that list. A hot drink should have also rated pretty well but as Jennifer's chuckle escaped she knew that the Tim Tam was enough for the time being.

And it was all they could do, the three of them, right now. To take each moment as it came and deal with it the best way they could.

Together.

'Yes, please,' she said softly into the darkness. 'I'd love a Tim Tam.'

CHAPTER THREE

THEY just had to get through the night.

'That red sunset meant it'll be a nice day tomorrow, didn't it?'

'Should be.' Guy wasn't making any promises.

'Shepherd's delight,' Digger said. 'It'll be clear.'

Clear skies with the wreck of a light plane glinting in sunshine on an exposed, rocky plateau. If they'd checked south of the great lakes already, they might well send someone looking to the north tomorrow. Maybe the locator beacon wasn't one of the faulty ones. Rescue would come.

They just had to get through the night. Right now, that seemed an achievable goal. It was cold, certainly, but it didn't feel dangerously so with the three of them huddled under the tarpaulin.

'The tussocks were a good idea.' Guy had used a pocket knife to slice off clumps of the strong mountain grass. It now provided a carpet for the floor of their shelter and insulation from the bone-chilling cold of the rocks beneath. 'Are you warm enough, Digger?'

'Feel like a chicken…ready for roasting.' Digger's breathing had a wheeze that was becoming steadily more audible, and he was still in enough respiratory distress to necessitate taking a breath after only a few words. 'Never been wrapped…in foil before.'

'You thirsty?' Guy's voice floated through the intense darkness.

'Yes. Very.' The sweetness of the chocolate biscuit

had been wonderful, but trying to swallow had made Jennifer realise just how thirsty she was.

'Actually, I was asking Digger. The snow I collected in this billy has finally melted.'

Jennifer bit back the automatic response that a patient awaiting surgery should be nil by mouth. It would be hours before they got Digger anywhere near an operating theatre. If they even managed to get him that far.

'Let Jenna have it...' Digger dragged in another breath. 'I'm fine.'

'Here it is, then.' Guy sounded resigned. 'I'll pass it round Digger's feet. I don't want to spill cold water on him.'

The foil sheet encasing Digger's legs crackled as Jennifer felt for direction. She could feel the warmth of Guy's hand well before she touched it, and she would rather have taken hold of his fingers than the cold metal container they held. There would be more comfort to be found in the touch of another person right now than in assuaging her thirst. She passed the billy back after just a few swallows.

'Can you pass me the torch?'

'Why?'

'I want to check the IV line and that bag of fluid.'

'I can do that.' The torch flashed briefly, running from the line in Digger's arm up to a bag that looked ominously flat. It wasn't quite empty, or blood would be visible, travelling back up the line, but it was going to run out pretty soon.

'Have you got the stethoscope on your side?'

'No.'

'OK.' Jennifer's hands left the protection of the inside of her anorak again and she felt around near Digger's head.

'Don't uncover him for any longer than you have to.'

'I'm not stupid, Guy.'

'I'm not doubting your intelligence,' he responded calmly. 'But I doubt that you've ever spent a night on a mountaintop before. It's going to get a lot colder than this, and we want to conserve all the heat we can.'

'Actually, I have spent a night on a mountaintop.'

'Where? In front of some après-ski open fire? A nicely exclusive resort in the Swiss Alps perhaps?'

'And you're an expert?' He wasn't so far from the truth, but why did he have to make it sound like she'd committed some kind of crime? Jennifer's hand curled around the stethoscope but she was now hesitant to expose Digger's chest to listen to his breath sounds.

'I know what I'm doing.'

'He does at that,' Digger said. 'We've had a few… dodgy nights…here and there.'

'Thanks to your desire to start a new gold rush.' Guy sounded as though he was smiling. 'We must have checked every obscure stream within tramping distance of every equally obscure airfield there is in these parts.'

'Are you a goldminer, Digger?'

'Just a…hobby.'

'Digger's a man of many talents,' Guy said quietly. 'Sheep shearer, rodeo king, deer hunter, top-dressing pilot, tavern manager and more recently a tour guide. He knows this country better than anyone.'

'Wish I…knew where…the bloody hell…we are… right…*now*…'

The difficulty he had in speaking had increased markedly. As Digger forced out the last vehement word he made a gagging sound and was suddenly silent.

'Digger?' Jennifer twisted onto her knees, her head scraping the canvas above her. She had the earpieces of her stethoscope fitted and was pulling away the covering on Digger's chest as Guy's shadow loomed behind the bright beam of the torch.

'We've lost any breath sounds on the left.'

'Digger?' Guy was unable to elicit any response. He swore under his breath.

'Help me unbandage this arm,' Jennifer directed. 'And then find a needle. I think that pneumothorax has finally tensioned.'

'I don't have a chest decompression needle in this kit.'

'A 12-gauge cannula will do. And a syringe.'

Unwrapping Digger's arm from where it was splinting his broken ribs was awkward enough in the cramped conditions. Shifting their patient so he was lying flat took precious seconds and finding the equipment she needed was frustratingly slow.

'I said a 12-gauge.'

'Fourteen's the best I've got.'

'I can't see a damn thing.'

'That's because you've got your head in the way.'

The canvas roof moved and Jennifer could hear a rock or two rolling away from anchoring their shelter as Guy moved further towards Digger's head and pointed the torch straight down.

Jennifer felt the ridges of Digger's ribs, counting to find the second intercostal space. Then she moved sideways until the needle tip was under the midpoint of the clavicle.

'OK, here we go.' She let the needle scrape over the top of the lower rib to avoid the bundle of nerves and veins beneath the higher rib. The pop as the tip pierced tissue over the air space could be heard as well as felt. Escaping air that had been trapped in the chest cavity, crushing the lung, came out in a hiss. 'Got it,' Jennifer said in relief. 'Let me have that syringe and I'll make sure I aspirate any more air or blood that's trapped.'

'What are you going to do with the needle?'

'I'll take it out and leave the catheter *in situ*. We'll cover it with an occlusive dressing but it may need aspirating again. He needs a tube thoracostomy as soon as possible.' Jennifer reached for the stethoscope but she could see that the lung was starting to function. The window of broken ribs was showing the disconcerting paradoxical movement again.

'We'd better get his arm splinting that again.'

'Hang on just a second.' Jennifer was positioning the disc of the stethoscope below Digger's clavicle. 'I'll listen to his chest and check his abdomen quickly first. How's his LOC looking?''

'He's coming round.'

Digger was conscious again by the time they had him propped back up, leaning towards his injured side. He was also in pain.

'I'll draw up another dose of morphine,' Guy decided. 'Your turn to hold the torch, Jenna.'

'Sure.' Jennifer flicked the beam upwards. 'We need to hang another bag of saline as well.'

Except it wasn't just *another* bag. It was the last bag, and it was going to be totally inadequate to replace the blood volume being lost internally if the increasing tension of Digger's abdomen was anything to go by. With the added stress of lacking oxygen due to respiratory distress, the shocked state Digger was already in would rapidly worsen. It was highly likely to become irreversible. And there wasn't a damned thing either of them could do about it.

The morphine made Digger a lot more comfortable, but his level of consciousness gradually decreased over the next hour or so. He could speak a little more freely now, but his thoughts were wandering and after a time of bitter self-recrimination for the accident and fatalities Digger seemed to forget where he was.

'I'll have a whisky, thanks, Di… Bloody cold tonight, eh?'

'Sure is.' Jennifer pulled the folds of the pale blue anorak more tightly around her and drew her knees up to her stomach. 'What time do you think it is, Guy?'

'I've no idea. I'll check my watch the next time we use the torch.'

'Ah…Diana,' Digger murmured. 'The goddess.'

'Who's he talking about?' Jennifer whispered.

'The woman he was in love with for years.'

'Oh?' Something in Guy's tone left a question unanswered.

'She was also my mother.'

'Oh.' Jennifer frowned in the darkness. 'So, is Digger your father, then?'

'Closest thing I ever had to one, anyway.'

'Stepfather?'

'No.' The conversation was clearly over and silence fell until Digger's voice startled them both.

'*Oi!* What the hell…do you think you're doing? Come here, you little bugger…and bring that back!'

'It's only us, Digger. Guy…and Jenna. We're here with you.' Guy's voice was reassuring but Digger seemed oblivious.

'I have to get up at sparrow's fart… I don't need some thieving kid…taking off with my smokes…'

'Smoking's bad for you, mate. You knew it was time to stop.'

'Don't need a snotty-nosed kid…telling me what to do… Just wait till I talk to…your mother…'

'Did you steal Digger's cigarettes?' Jennifer found herself smiling. 'Were you on a crusade or trying a life of crime?'

'I was only twelve. A life of crime seemed a good idea at the time.'

Guy was probably in his mid-thirties now, so he had known Digger for a very long time. A father figure. Jennifer remembered the glimpse of anguish she had seen on Guy's face when he'd first confronted the extent of Digger's injuries. Now he was lying close to someone he loved, and that person was dying. As if to emphasise her bleak thoughts, Digger mumbled something completely incoherent and lapsed into silence. Jennifer swallowed hard.

'I'm sorry,' she said quietly into the darkness a minute or two later.

'What for?'

'That I can't do more to help Digger.'

There was a long hesitation before the response came. 'Not half as sorry as I am.'

Jennifer shrank a little further into the folds of her anorak as the depth of feeling in his words echoed in her head. Had that been a personal slight? Did he expect a consultant in emergency medicine to be able to perform some kind of miracle? She shook her head, dispelling the faintly paranoid notion. Given the bond that existed between these men, it was far more likely that the comment was a bitter reflection on his own inability to provide assistance.

The sounds of Digger's breathing filled the tiny tent. How long would his injured lungs manage to struggle on, trying to provide enough oxygen to keep cells alive? Jennifer looked upwards. She couldn't see the bag of saline in the darkness but she could picture the steady drip of fluid entering Digger's veins. It was such inadequate treatment for the condition he was in.

If the internal bleeding continued, he would enter irreversible shock within the next few hours. Lack of oxygen-carrying red cells would cause the major organs like kidneys and heart and brain to fail. If they had been in an emergency department, it would be so easy to do what was needed. X-rays and ultrasound. Aggressive fluid replacement. A proper chest decompression. A quick trip to Theatre to have the source of the abdominal blood loss fixed.

The isolation of their situation was suddenly overwhelming because it was going to cause someone's death, and there was absolutely nothing Jennifer could do about it. Her sigh was heartfelt.

'What's the matter?'

'Nothing.' Nothing new, anyway. Jennifer sighed again. 'Everything,' she corrected herself. 'This is *so* frustrating. I know what should be done and there's no way of doing it. It's…just *awful.*'

'You must be pretty used to awful things. How many cases a day would you put through your ED? Dozens? Hundreds?'

'Somewhere in between. But that's different. Sure, we lose patients and it's awful sometimes, but at least we've done everything we could and we get to save people who wouldn't make it without us. People like Digger.'

The silence suggested that Guy didn't want to discuss Digger's obviously bleak prognosis. When he spoke, he almost sounded as though he was having a conversation at a cocktail party.

'So, what's the most awful case you've ever had to deal with?'

'It's never nice to lose a patient. You must know that.'

'It's different for me. I know most of my patients on a personal basis. Even something as mundane as a cardiac arrest is awful, but it doesn't happen too often fortunately. You'd get far more interesting things to deal with. So what's the worst you can think of?'

'This isn't exactly a happy topic of conversation.'

'Maybe I don't feel happy,' Guy responded. 'Or maybe I need to think about other people who are even less fortunate than me. I'm curious anyway. You have a very different perspective on medicine than I do these days, so it must take something pretty major to stand out as being memorably awful. Humour me. What constitutes *really* awful for you?'

This, Jennifer wanted to say. Lying beside someone who could be saved and isn't going to be. Having the person who probably loves him more than any other lying on the other side. Being connected by their physical proximity and the enormity of their predicament. Knowing that when there was absolutely nothing more they could do for Digger, the distraction of caring for someone else would be lost and she would have to face the fear of her own chances of survival.

Instead, she drew in a deep breath and spoke quietly. 'There was this woman a couple of years ago. Lucy, her name was. She was thirty-five and she and her husband had been desperate to have a baby for years. It took about six attempts but IVF finally worked and she became pregnant with twins. Seven and a half months pregnant. They went out shopping for a double buggy and while they were walking along a path, Lucy spotted this puppy in a pet-shop window. She stopped abruptly and turned to have a look, but this kid had been coming up behind on a skateboard and he barrelled into her.'

Jennifer paused to take another breath. Digger mumbled something and jerked his head but then lay still again.

'And?' Guy prompted. 'What happened? Did she miscarry?'

'No. She stumbled and fell sideways into the path of a car. Severe head injury but she was still alive when she arrived in ED. She arrested shortly after arrival so I decided to do an emergency Caesarean to try and save the babies. Her husband, Matt, was right outside the door of the resus room.'

Even now, the memory was enough to create a painful lump in her throat. What had she been thinking of, agreeing to tell such an awful story? Jennifer blinked hard and doggedly carried on.

'It was a circus. We had dozens of people rushing in and out. We had to tube Lucy and keep CPR going. We had obstetric and paediatric and neurology staff arriving, and every time the door swung open Matt got a glimpse of what was going on. He saw his wife being cut open and his babies being resuscitated. And then...then I had to go and tell him that we had failed. He'd lost everyone—his whole family. His whole reason for living.'

Long seconds ticked by before Guy broke the new silence. 'That's worse than awful,' he said finally. 'It's a truly heartbreaking story.'

'You did ask,' Jennifer reminded him.

'OK, so tell me about the best case you've ever had,' he commanded.

'There's been lots of those as well.' Jennifer was thankful to turn her thoughts to something positive. Maybe the reminder of just how dreadful events could be for others hadn't been such a bad thing after all. 'One of my favourites was a three-year-old girl who came in under CPR. She had fallen into a river but we weren't sure whether she'd arrested because of drowning or hypothermia. It was the middle of winter and she was unbelievably cold.'

'A "not dead until you're warm and dead" case?' Guy suggested.

'Absolutely. It took thirty minutes to get her core temperature above 30 degrees Celsius and she was still in asystole. Her parents were quite convinced she was dead. We defibrillated her finally. It took three goes but we got her back.'

'Brain damaged?'

'No.' Jennifer was smiling into the darkness. 'She came into the department a week later with her parents, carrying a big bunch of flowers for me.'

'Have you got kids of your own?'

'No.'

'Planning on some?'

'That's a rather personal question. Why—are you?'

'Definitely not.'

'You sound very sure about that.'

'I am. I like my life just the way it is. There's no space for kids in it.'

'So what makes you assume *I* want a family?' Jennifer was frowning. *Did* she want a family? It wasn't something that had been more than a fleeting thought over the years. A thought that was easy to shove on the back burner due to the precedence her career had always taken. 'Not all women are born with the desperate need to reproduce. Maybe I'm just as sure about it as you are.'

'You just gave me the impression that you're fond of kids, that's all.'

'How on earth did you reach a conclusion like that?'

'Both your worst and best cases involved babies and children.'

'I guess those cases can be more memorable. Maybe it's more of a tragedy to lose babies and children than older people who have had a chance to live life.'

'Like Digger, you mean?'

'No, I didn't mean that.' Jennifer's tone softened. 'Digger's obviously special. He reminds me of my dad.'

'Because he called you Jenna?'

'Not just that. There's something else there. An independence maybe. Or courage, or a sense of humour. An ability to face whatever has to be faced without making a big fuss about it.'

Guy grunted. 'You're not a bad judge of character.' Jennifer could hear him moving. 'Hey, Digger? Did you hear the nice things Dr Allen was saying about you?'

There was no response from Digger. Jennifer moved as well, to wriggle her hand inside the coverings and find Digger's wrist.

'His radial pulse isn't palpable,' she said quietly. 'Blood pressure's dropping.'

'He's not responsive,' Guy added. 'And I don't like how shallow and rapid his breathing's getting.'

Digger was tilted towards Guy's side of the tent and as Jennifer was tucking his arm back under the leather jacket and foil sheet she found him tilting even further. Startled, Jennifer opened her mouth to say something but then realised what was happening. Guy was taking the older man into his arms.

'It's OK, mate,' he was saying softly. 'I'm here, Digger. I'm not going anywhere.'

This time tears formed that rolled down Jennifer's face. Would someone hold her like that when she was dying? And speak softly in such a loving tone? There

was a gap beside her now, where Digger's back
had been.

'Come a bit closer,' Guy instructed. 'We need to keep
as much body heat in one place as we can. Pull the tarp
in around us if you can.'

So Jennifer found herself pressed against Digger's
back again. She could feel his uneven breathing beneath
her cheek. She could feel the erratic heartbeat a long
time later when his breathing settled into a rhythm that
suggested the end wasn't far away. They huddled together as the minutes, then hours passed. The cold was
numbing and attempts at conversation gradually faded
into simply waiting.

Waiting for dawn.

Waiting for rescue.

Sadly, there would be no rescue for Jim Spade. As
the inky blackness outside lightened by slow degrees
into a frigid dawn, Digger took his last breath and
slipped away, held in the circle of Guy's and Jennifer's
arms. Neither of them could break the contact immediately and Jennifer had no idea how long they lay like
that. It was Guy who struggled free first. He laid Digger
gently on his back and then turned and wriggled out of
the tent. When Jennifer put her head outside the shelter
she found the light strong enough to see the silhouette
of the man standing some distance away on the edge of
the plateau.

The craggy rock faces of the more distant peaks provided a backdrop for the solitary figure. A figure whose
head was bent and shoulders were shaking in grief.
Jennifer closed her eyes and buried her face in her hands.
She knew neither of these men in any real sense, yet she
felt as bad as she had on her father's recent death. Her
heart ached for Guy and she had to resist the impulse to

go and offer comfort of some kind. He had gone as far
away from the tent—and her—as he possibly could, so
he clearly needed some time alone. He would come back
when he was ready and Jennifer would do her very best
to comfort him if she could.

Except that Guy didn't want to be offered any comfort.
When he finally returned to the shelter, the first rays of
sunlight were lifting the temperature just enough to be
noticeable. The coldest thing Jennifer was aware of had
to be the expression on Guy's face.

'I'm so sorry, Guy,' she said softly.

'You didn't even know him.' The tone dismissed any
right Jennifer had to show empathy.

'That doesn't stop me feeling bad. For Digger…and
you.'

'I don't need your sympathy.' Guy folded back the
tarpaulin from where Jennifer was huddled in the entrance to the shelter. 'I'm going to need this,' he muttered. 'If it gets windy or wet, you can get inside what's
left of the plane for shelter.'

'What?' Jennifer watched in bemusement as Guy laid
the canvas square on the ground and started putting
items on top of it. The billy, his pocket knife, a length
of rope. He took off the dark blue anorak and replaced
it with his leather jacket. Jennifer had taken it off Digger
when she had covered him completely with one of the
foil sheets. Guy seemed to be ignoring the sight of the
shrouded body of his friend. He took the spare foil sheet
and added it to the pile on the tarpaulin.

'What are you doing?' His actions were making Jennifer
nervous.

'Packing.'

'Why? Have you seen something?' Jennifer turned her

gaze to the horizon. The blue of the sky was becoming brighter and the day was as clear as she could have wished, but she could see nothing that suggested rescue was at hand.

'I'm going to walk out and get help.' Guy picked up the half-eaten packet of chocolate biscuits and put them down beside Jennifer. 'You can keep these.'

'You can't *leave!*' Jennifer was horrified. 'The first rule for anybody lost in the bush is to stay put. Even *I* know that.'

'I know what I'm doing.'

'We're on the top of a mountain, for God's sake! There's no way you can *walk* out.'

'It'll take a while,' Guy agreed calmly. 'Three days at the most to get to civilisation, I reckon. I've been having a good look. The climbing's a bit tricky to get down to the bush line but I've picked out a route I think I can manage. I might find a river in the next valley and I should be able to follow that to get somewhere recognisable. I know this country pretty well. I'll survive.' He rolled up the items in the canvas. 'If they find you first, you can let them know what I was planning.'

'*If* they find me first?'

'There's no guarantee they'll come looking in the right place. I'm not going to sit up here for days getting hypothermic and dehydrated and then decide to try and walk out.'

'You can't leave me.' Jennifer's voice rose sharply. 'I'm not going to sit here with three dead people all by myself.'

For the first time since he'd returned to the shelter, Guy turned to look at Digger. A long moment passed and Jennifer kicked herself mentally for seeming uncaring enough to have made Digger simply one of the fatalities. Guy turned away abruptly.

'I'm going,' he said flatly. 'You can't stop me.'

'Then I'll come with you.'

'Ha!' The sound was scathing. 'Don't be ridiculous. You wouldn't make it past the first ridge.'

'What makes you so sure about that?'

Guy just looked at her and Jennifer had never felt so inadequate in her life. She didn't know what scared her more—attempting a journey that would probably be impossible or sitting here alone, waiting for rescue that might, conceivably, never come.

'Do you want to go rock-climbing? Fording rivers? Forcing yourself through bush that could be virtually impenetrable?'

'No! Of course I don't. And you shouldn't either. If you get lost out there, it'll be the end. At least we're visible here. They'll be looking for a plane.'

'I'll mark my route.'

'You can't do this!' Jennifer shook her head, feeling horribly close to crying and begging him to stay. 'What about your leg? Your ankle? How far do you think you'll get on that?'

'As far as I need to,' Guy said grimly. 'I'm going to see if I can unearth your cell phone in the plane. The battery on mine is dead. It's possible I can come across a spot on a ridge that might give some coverage. There might even be a hut with a radio somewhere along the way.'

'A hut?' Jennifer caught her bottom lip in her teeth. Was that really possible? If they had the shelter of a hut, survival was far more likely.

'We're in a national park. I'm not sure exactly where, but there are a lot of tracks used by trampers and climbers in the area. With a bit of luck I might come across one of them in a day or two.' Guy crouched beside the red bag as he spoke. 'I'll take a few bandages and a clean dressing or two, though. What do you need me to leave for your arm?'

'My arm's fine.' Jennifer wasn't even aware of the discomfort now. She had too much else to worry about. She followed Guy as he went back to the wreckage of the plane.

'You can't do this,' she insisted. 'You have to stay put. Everybody knows that's what you're supposed to do when you're lost.'

'Only if you don't know what you're doing,' Guy countered. 'Like you.' He eventually had to give up the search for Jennifer's handbag and he straightened and met her gaze directly for the first time since Digger's death.

'You'll be all right,' he said. 'Keep yourself as warm as you can and melt some snow for water. I'll leave you the extra jacket. You could take some more clothing off Bill and Shirley as well and put that on.' Something like concern flashed momentarily in his gaze. 'I'll get help just as fast as I can.'

And then, with what seemed like total incongruity, he smiled. 'See you in a few days, Jenna.'

Jennifer watched him walk away. Saw him stoop to collect the rolled tarpaulin and then keep walking. He reached the edge of the plateau, where he'd stood so long alone at dawn, and stopped for several seconds, perhaps confirming the route he wanted to take. With one hand on a huge boulder for support, he then stepped lower. Another step and his hand left the rock. A second later his head disappeared from view.

He was gone.

Jennifer had never felt more alone in her life. Even her mother's death, when she'd only been eight, hadn't left her feeling this bereft. Or losing her only remaining family when her father had died so many years later. Feeling the last breath Digger had taken so recently had brought back too many memories of loss, and seeing Guy disappear over the edge of the plateau was too much.

Jennifer didn't want to die. She especially didn't want to die alone. And she was damned if she wasn't going to do something to try and help herself. If Guy believed he could make it, there was no reason why she couldn't keep up with him. Maybe they'd both die in the attempt, but at least they wouldn't be giving up.

And they wouldn't be alone.

She had no real choice in the end. It felt good to move—to make some decisions.

'Sorry, Shirley.' Jennifer had to grit her teeth to approach the dead woman. 'I need to borrow your shoes and trousers. I don't think a skirt and high heels are going to help me get very far.'

Having made the decision, it became urgent. Trying to cope with shoelaces and zips with frozen hands and a half-splinted arm seemed to take far too long. When she had put on the second jacket on top of her odd collection of garments, Jennifer stumbled in her haste to get to the edge of the plateau.

She stopped by the boulder where she had last seen Guy, and her hand went out for support. It wasn't the first stage of climbing down, however. She needed the support to cope with what she was seeing. The steep, snow-covered drop was pierced only infrequently by visible rock formations. It looked totally impossible to cross and it didn't lead, as she had expected, to the sight of a forest and a potentially manageable route. As far as she could see there were more ridges and plateaus with only snow, rock and grass tussocks. The bush line was miles away, lower than her by what looked like thousands of feet.

Where was Guy? Jennifer squinted against the glare of the sun on snow. Close to her feet she could see the prints he had left in the snow. Every second one seemed noticeably deeper, as though he was favouring his injured ankle. Her eyes tracked the line, crossed a rocky area and just picked up the marks again on the other side.

Raising her gaze a little, she spotted him. How had he gone so far in such a short time? He was halfway across the slope, heading sideways, not straight down. Of course, Jennifer thought, he'd be doing some kind of zigzag to get down safely. And if he'd gone this far in the time it had taken her to follow then maybe there was hope. The day was clear and there were many hours of daylight left.

He knew what he was doing.

Jennifer clung to the thought as she stepped down to the snow. She put her feet into the prints Guy had left, stretching her stride to match the steps he had taken. The scramble over the first patch of rocks was terrifying but Jennifer forced herself to continue. She found a handhold with her uninjured arm and then a place for each foot. Then she was into the snow again, with Guy's prints to guide her and provide reassurance that she wouldn't slip to her death.

'I can do this,' she found herself saying aloud. 'I can make it. Wait for me, Guy. *Please!*'

CHAPTER FOUR

SHE was *following* him.

It had taken several incredulous seconds for Guy to figure out what the moving blob on the snow near the rocks above and behind him was, and when he did, he swore aloud and kept moving.

This was the *last* thing he needed. The risk he was taking was huge but he was experienced. To have the liability of someone like Jennifer trailing after him spelled almost certain failure. He would have the concern of her safety hanging around his neck like a millstone, adding unwanted and probably overwhelming weight to every decision he would have to make. At best, she would slow him down enough to tip the balance against surviving. At worst, she could cause both their deaths.

Guy kept his gaze on the next outcrop of rock he was heading towards. He kicked the next step into the layer of snow with his heel, testing its firmness before allowing his whole weight to follow and praying that his injured ankle would take the strain yet again and not collapse and send him hurtling downwards like a human avalanche. He was moving sideways and down the vast slope. One step and then another.

He could just keep going, couldn't he, and pretend he hadn't seen her? He could probably increase his pace considerably once he got past this icy slope and then she would never catch up.

She'll die, a voice in his head stated clearly. *Is that what you want?*

'Of course not,' Guy muttered. 'But she'll probably die anyway and take me down with her. She should have stayed where she was. I would have sent help...eventually.'

You weren't too keen to stay, were you? the voice taunted. *With three dead people for company? With* Digger?

'I couldn't.' The pain was still too great. A raw wound that was unbearable.

Maybe she *couldn't either.*

'She didn't even know him.'

She tried to save his life. She said he reminded her of her father. You knew she'd been crying when you went back. She cared.

Guy refused to respond to that one. She had no right to care and he didn't want anyone claiming even a tiny share of his pain. Especially a total stranger.

Where the hell was this voice coming from? Was he already hypothermic and dehydrated and exhausted enough that his brain function was impaired? He couldn't afford to doubt himself right now. He needed to concentrate on what he was doing and ignore any negative thoughts.

The voice wasn't about to give up so easily.

What would Digger think of what you're trying to do? it whispered.

'He'd do exactly what I'm doing. Take a risk and go for help.'

He wouldn't have left someone behind. Someone who had tried to save the life of someone he loved. Someone who cared.

'Dammit!' Guy snarled. 'Dammit it to hell!' He had

reached the rocky outcrop. Two sections of his zigzag descent completed safely. And now he had to wait.

To wait until Jennifer bloody Allen caught up with him. And then he'd have to drag her along and try and keep them both alive until they reached help because otherwise his conscience, or whatever was creating that persistent voice, would probably plague him for the rest of his life.

'I would have waited anyway,' he growled aloud. 'I just wanted to get to the rocks so I could sit down for a minute.'

It took more like twenty minutes for Jennifer to catch up.

'Just what the *hell* do you think you're *doing?*' Guy might have been planning to wait all along, but there was no way he was going to applaud her rash decision.

'I'm coming with you.'

'You're out of your mind. Go back and stay with the plane.'

'No way. I've come this far. I'm not turning back now.'

'And just how far do you think you're going to get?'

'As far as I need to,' Jennifer flashed back. 'Just like you.'

'You'll never make it.' She had already made an effort, though, hadn't she? Guy shook his head to stop that voice speaking on her behalf.

His gaze raked her from head to foot and a breath escaped in a huff that was verging on laughter. She looked ridiculous. They must be Shirley's trousers she was wearing. Or even Bill's. They looked several sizes too big and she still had her skirt on top of them. Wearing two anoraks made her look like a child who'd been layered up in hand-me-down protective clothing to go out and build a snowman, and the lace-up suede shoes she had swapped her high heels for were already soaked. She have frostbite in no time flat if they stayed above the snow line.

'I'm sorry,' he said with even more emphasis. 'But you can't manage this.'

'You don't know that.'

'I know that you have no idea what you're trying to get into. I'll bet the biggest physical challenge you've faced recently is a Pilates class.'

'Don't judge me when you don't even know me.' Jennifer had her hands tucked inside her jacket, hugging her body for warmth.

'I know your type,' Guy told her mercilessly. 'For God's sake, go back. I'll be a lot quicker without you. I'll send help.'

'No. I'm not going back.'

'I can't carry you out of here. It's simply not possible.'

'I'm not asking you to.'

'I'm not going to sit and wait for you every time you fall behind.'

'I'm not asking you to do that either. I'll keep up.'

'It's going to get a damned sight harder than what you've managed so far.'

He saw the flash of fear. She turned her head to glance downwards and shut her eyes briefly as though it was too much to contemplate.

Great. She was scared out of her wits already. What was going to happen when they reached some real rock-climbing that had to be faced? Or a swollen river that needed crossing?

Then he caught another glimpse of clear blue eyes as Jennifer turned her gaze upwards, covering the route she had just taken to follow him as far as she had. Her chin came up and gaze met his squarely.

'I can do this,' she stated quietly. 'Just watch.'

Guy snorted. 'I'll be looking ahead,' he said. 'Not over my shoulder.'

'Fine.' Jennifer's gaze was as unrelenting as he knew his must be. 'What are you waiting for, then?'

They had to get across the snow-covered slope at least once more. Below that, clumps of tussocks broke through and there were areas of rock that were clear of snow.

'Dig your heels in,' Guy ordered. 'And keep your weight over your feet. You'll lose your balance if you lean in towards the slope.'

He moved forward doggedly, kicking steps that he only hoped she had the sense to use herself. It was impossible not to keep glancing back, and every time he did, he found she was only a metre or two behind. She had her gaze fixed firmly on the ground in front of her feet and her face was set in grim lines. She was determined, he had to give her that.

The silence seemed to get louder as it stretched on. Kicking steps in snow was hard work, and Guy was forced to stop and catch his breath when they were only halfway through the next leg of this descent. He cleared his throat.

'If you fall,' he said, 'you'll have to do something to save yourself pretty quickly or you'll be history. Roll onto your stomach and dig your hands in if you need to in order to face uphill. You lift yourself into a ''press-up'' position and then dig your hands and feet into the snow as hard as you can.'

'Cool.' Jennifer was also trying to catch her breath

but her tone indicated a valiant attempt to sound non-chalant. 'Just as well they taught press-ups in my Pilates class, isn't it?'

By the time they were on the last leg of traversing the snow-covered gully, Jennifer's confidence had grown considerably.

She could do this. She could see past the rocks bordering the sides at the base of the gully now, and before long they would reach an area that looked inviting by comparison. The rock face was a far more gentle slope created by an uneven series of steps, with patches of grass and even the cheerful bloom of mountain buttercups. The sun was shining brightly now and Jennifer actually felt too hot in her multiple layers of clothing.

They'd be able to stop for a well-earned rest, melt snow for water and maybe finish the packet of chocolate biscuits stuffed into the pocket of her oversized outer anorak. Optimism bloomed as cheerfully as the clumps of flowers ahead, and Jennifer turned her head to look back up the gully. Some self-congratulation was surely overdue considering how terrifying it had been to begin this journey and how well she had coped so far.

Looking up was a big mistake. Her foot missed the print Guy had left, the rock beneath the thinner patch of snow she trod on was as slippery as ice and Jennifer fell so quickly she had no idea what had happened until she hit the ground.

There was a slope of only about ten to fifteen metres to where the ground levelled out, but it was too far to slide at speed without injuring oneself badly on the rocks below. Jennifer dug her hands into the snow and cried out at the pain that shot up her left arm. She still forced it to take her weight, however, as she remembered Guy's advice and tried to push herself up and get her body off the snow. She bent her feet as well, driving her toes down.

Snow filled her open mouth, went up her nose and scorched her cheeks. Then her hip bumped painfully on something solid, but her slide was arrested. Jennifer found herself on her knees a second later, spitting out snow and scrubbing at her eyes to clear her vision.

What she saw was Guy turning back to the path he was taking. He must have stopped on hearing her cry out, watched long enough to confirm she hadn't caused herself any grievous bodily harm and now he was pressing on without taking the time to see whether she needed any help. He'd meant what he'd said, hadn't he? He wasn't going to stop and wait for her every time she fell behind. She was an unwanted liability and if he'd had any choice he would have made sure she'd stayed behind with the plane wreckage.

Jennifer sat on the snow for several seconds, watching Guy pick his way cautiously across the remaining slope. She looked down. A manageable-looking gradient ended with a large, flat-sided rock several metres below where the snow petered out. With only a momentary hesitation, Jennifer stuck her feet out and pushed off with her good hand. The speed she gathered was no more than her bent legs could easily absorb when she reached the rock and then she could get to her feet and start walking. She would actually be ahead of Guy by the time he reached the flatter ground, which suited her just fine.

He hadn't been going to wait for her. He clearly didn't give a damn whether she'd been injured or not by her fall. He would probably be glad of an excuse to just leave her behind and press on by himself. Well, he had a thing or two to learn, didn't he? He had no idea how tough she was and he had no right to despise her 'type'—whatever the hell he'd meant by that. Waiting for Guy to catch up with her right now was quite possibly the most satisfying moment in her life. She even tossed back a few strands of damp blonde hair.

'What took you so long, then?'

The look Jennifer received could only be described as withering. Then Guy snorted softly and shook his head. He unhooked the coil of rope that held the tarpaulin to his shoulder and set the bundle down on top of the nearest rock.

'I'm going to melt some snow,' he said. 'Eating it isn't a good idea. It can give you abdominal pain and dry out your mouth.'

Jennifer made no response to what appeared to be an oblique reference to her fall. Guy was undoing the rope.

'I've got a bit of black plastic in here from the survival kit. It'll melt snow in this sunshine in no time.' He positioned the billy, put a handful of snow onto the plastic and then glanced up at Jennifer. 'Come and hold this,' he instructed. 'Point it down at the corner so the melting snow goes into the billy.'

'OK.' It looked ingenious to Jennifer. 'I've got the rest of the biscuits. Do you want one?'

'In a minute.' Guy pushed back the sleeve of his jacket to unbuckle his wristwatch. 'I'm going to try and figure out what direction we need to head in.'

The billy was half full by the time Guy stopped squinting at the sun, adjusting his hold on the wristwatch and staring off towards the horizon.

'I think I might have a rough idea of where we are,' he said.

'Great,' Jennifer responded. 'Where are we?'

'Somewhere in the Balfour Range, I think. On the western side toward Cook Valley. The Copland Range should be somewhere south of where we are.' Guy's hand swung to a point at right angles to where he had indicated south. 'That's Mount Cook you can see way over there.'

'It's a very long way away.' Jennifer stared at the section of the Southern Alps visible over the endless spurs and ridges that filled the immediate horizon.

'We're not heading that way. If we head south, we might come across a track. Even a hut, if we're lucky. Some of the trampers' huts have radios. They all have logbooks and maps anyway, so at least we'd know exactly where we were.' He rubbed a hand over his chin, staring off into the distance again. 'Not that we'll be able to take a direct route and I won't be able to navigate by the stars as well as I can with the sun and my watch, so we'll have to stop once it gets dark.' He reached for the billy. 'Have you had something to drink?'

'Yes, thanks.' Jennifer's gaze was fixed on Guy. Had he really intended to keep walking, day and night, without stopping to rest properly? She couldn't have done that, no matter how determined she might be.

'We should both get at least a litre on board before we head off again. We won't find so much snow soon and we'll have to hope we come across a lake or stream to get more water.'

Guy drank and Jennifer found herself watching the movement of his Adam's apple as he swallowed. His chin and neck were already roughened by dark stubble and he had lost none of the grime and streaks of blood since yesterday. He looked as though he could spend time tramping day and night over mountains just for fun, and his expression, as he lowered the billy, was as grim as the surrounding terrain. If he was a stranger that Jennifer was seeing for the first time, she decided, he'd be terrifying. Then, unexpectedly, Guy's lips curved to one side and even half a smile softened his features so dramatically Jennifer found herself smiling back.

'I hope you haven't scoffed all those Tim Tams,' he said. 'I'm starving.'

The renewed energy provided by the shared but totally inadequate meal was short-lived. Jennifer had to keep pushing herself not to fall too far behind. Guy led the way towards the next spur. And the next. Her arm hurt. Her feet started to hurt as well. Shirley's shoes may have been far better than her high heels for this trek, but the other woman's feet were at least two sizes bigger than her own and her feet slipped inside the suede lace-ups as she walked.

Blisters were forming and Jennifer had to simply ignore the pain and carry on. If Guy could keep up this kind of pace with only a minimal limp from favouring what had to be at the very least a badly sprained ankle, she could just imagine what his reaction would be if she complained of a blister. It would probably rank alongside a broken fingernail as an injury someone of her 'type' would find ridiculously significant.

Every so often she had the chance to close the gap between them a little because Guy would pause and tie a knot in a tussock.

'Why are you doing that?' Jennifer asked on the second occasion.

'I'm marking our route.' Guy twisted the tough mountain grass and then tugged it into a thick bundle. 'The prints we left in the snow will be clearly visible if it doesn't snow again. If a search and rescue team gets winched in to follow us, I want to make sure they come the right way.'

Jennifer wouldn't have thought of that. The only lore for those lost in the wild she had retained was that you stayed put, and they had broken that rule some time ago. She wondered what other survival gems Guy had available, but the exchange about the knotted grass was the only conversation that took place for a very long stretch of time.

The silence as they walked was almost as distressing as any physical discomfort. Jennifer worked very long hours in one of the busiest emergency departments in the country. She lived in a central city apartment above a trendy shopping precinct that never completely closed. Her world was never silent and never lonely, and that was exactly the way she liked it.

The oppressive quiet of their surroundings and any lack of companionship didn't seem to bother Guy at all. Even when they stopped for a short rest, he simply dropped the bundle he was carrying beside Jennifer and then walked off to do his thing with his watch and the sun again.

Jennifer's voice sounded loud in the silence. 'So how do you navigate by using your watch?'

'You point the figure 12 towards the sun. True north is approximately halfway between 12 and the hour hand.'

'Too bad if you've got a digital watch, then.'

The raised eyebrows were enough to make Jennifer realise she'd missed the point. She sighed. 'OK. I guess as long as you have the correct time, you know where the hands should be.'

Guy's expression and brief nod were the kind of acknowledgement a parent might make to a child who had said something unexpectedly clever. Jennifer found herself increasingly annoyed by his condescension as she once again trailed in Guy's footsteps. He had some nerve!

They both knew how dependent she currently was on his skills. Wasn't that enough to allow him to feel superior without taking other opportunities to put her down? He'd already made it clear he didn't like her and she wasn't that thrilled with his personality either, but it shouldn't matter what they thought of each other on a personal or professional level.

They were in this together, and it would be nice to be recognised as an active participant and not simply a passenger. Surely she deserved some credit for keeping up? It had to be time for another rest. Hours had passed since they'd eaten the biscuits, and shadows in the valley were lengthening. The temperature dropped steadily as the sun lowered but still Guy went steadily on.

When he did stop, it was abruptly enough for Jennifer not to notice until she bumped into him.

'Sorry!'

His arm had caught hers, which was just enough to stop her toppling from exhaustion. 'You can stop for a bit,' he said. 'I think we've found a good place to camp for the night. Look at that!'

Jennifer's gaze had been on Guy's back or the track in front of her feet for so long she had to blink to focus. Then her jaw dropped.

'It's gorgeous!' she exclaimed.

The mountain lake ahead was so still it reflected the surrounding peaks absolute perfectly. Trees grew close to one side where a stream led into the bush line.

'We'll head for that stream,' Guy announced. 'We'll build a shelter among the big boulders and I should be able to get a fire going with some fuel from the bush.'

It sounded like heaven to Jennifer, but having stopped

it was an effort to force her feet to move again and when she did it was impossible not to limp.

Guy said nothing until they had gone another five hundred metres to where huge boulders were overhung by the branches of massive trees.

'I'll start collecting some wood, shall I?' Jennifer offered. 'For the fire?'

Guy shook his head. 'Sit down,' he ordered. 'I want to look at your feet.'

'I'm fine,' Jennifer protested. Then she looked up and caught Guy's expression and she was suddenly way too tired and sore to try arguing. Or even to care that she was so dependent on this man who thought she was a waste of space. She sat.

Guy pulled at the wet laces on her shoes. 'These things are like boats on your feet,' he said. 'I don't know how you've managed to walk as far as you have today.'

'How far do you think we've come?'

Guy eased a shoe off. 'Somewhere between ten and fifteen kilometres. A good distance over this kind of terrain anyway. Especially for someone who isn't used to this kind of thing.' He pulled a sock off before he glanced up. 'Well done, Jenna. I'm impressed.'

The glow of pride created almost as much warmth as her feet were generating under the cool touch of Guy's hands.

'What a mess!' he said in disgust.

Jennifer had to agree. Her feet were bright red, alarmingly swollen and had angry raw patches where blisters had long since popped and rubbed away.

'Soak them in the stream for a minute or two,' Guy suggested. 'We've got extra dressings and bandages and hopefully we'll have a fire going soon so we can warm you up if they get too cold.'

Jennifer sat on a rock, easing her burning feet by degrees into what felt like liquid ice as she watched Guy gather materials for a fire. He disappeared into the bush briefly and came back with an armload of twigs and bark. He gathered small pieces of driftwood from the stony edge of the lake and then glanced towards Jennifer.

'I'll just go and find some bigger pieces,' he told her. 'Won't be long.'

The sound of him moving through the undergrowth ceased astonishingly quickly. Jennifer heard the loud snap of a branch from further away and then only silence. She twisted to look at the forest but it was becoming rapidly dark and forbidding. Twisting further, she turned her gaze to the mirror created by the small lake, and she could see the sunset gilding the mountain peaks without raising her eyes any further.

For a moment the thought of Guy somewhere in the forest behind her vanished, and Jennifer realised she was more alone than she had ever been in her life. Strangely, it wasn't frightening. The beauty around her was awe-inspiring and the sense of being so insignificant ceased to matter because she wasn't trying to impose herself on this landscape in any way. She was simply a part of it for those few minutes. A part of something breathtakingly magnificent. And what should have been overwhelming enough to inspire fear gave Jennifer a sense of utter peace instead.

The moment was lost as she heard Guy return and saw his arms laden with wood.

'You look exhausted,' he said.

'I think I must be.' Jennifer summoned a smile. 'I was actually enjoying the view.'

Guy just grunted. He crouched low and started arranging his supplies. With the pocket knife he'd used last night to harvest grass, he shaved fine slivers from a piece of driftwood, covering a handful of dead leaves. He used a cigarette lighter to start the fire.

'Someone must be on our side,' he murmured. 'This would be so much harder if it had been raining.'

Jennifer watched the smoke curling up from the leaves, then the tiny flicker of flames reaching for the kindling Guy added slowly. When he was satisfied the fire was well alight, he filled the billy with water from the stream and balanced it on top of the fire. Then he turned his attention to Jennifer's feet.

His hands felt deliciously warm against her chilled skin now. Warm...and very gentle.

'Wiggle your toes,' he commanded. 'Now your ankles. Does anything hurt?'

'They feel better now they've had a rest.'

'The swelling's gone down quite a lot.' Guy took the bag of first-aid supplies and smeared antiseptic cream over the raw patches before covering them with gauze dressings. Then he sliced a crêpe bandage in half lengthways to make a narrow strip, which he used to bind the dressings in place. 'This should work like extra socks,' he commented. 'Might make the shoes fit a bit better as well. Now.' He sat back on his heels. 'Let's see that arm.'

The cardboard splint had become soggy way back when the snow had gone up her sleeve that morning. It was doing little to support the fracture but Jennifer's arm still felt exposed and vulnerable when the splint was removed along with the bandage.

'Any paresthesia?' Guy queried.

'A bit,' Jennifer admitted. 'Just in the tips of my ring and little fingers.' The tingling had started after that fall.

'Can you squeeze my hand?'

His fingers felt wonderfully warm and solid. Jennifer closed her hand around them and held on. It was worth the pain.

'Pretty weak,' Guy grunted. 'You'll have to watch you don't trust any real weight on that arm tomorrow.' He uncurled her fingers and removed his hand. 'I'll find a stick or two we can splint it with. That cardboard's useless.'

'What about your ankle?' Jennifer asked when he returned. 'And that nasty cut on your leg?'

'They'll keep.' Guy bound her arm firmly. 'I'm going to collect some leaves for the base of our shelter and then…' He smiled at Jennifer '…I'm going to make the best soup you've ever tasted in your life.'

It was more like faintly chicken-flavoured hot water, with only two packets of dehydrated soup dissolved in a whole billy full of boiling water, but Guy was right. It was more delicious than anything Jennifer could remember. The thin layer of noodles at the bottom was a bonus. They took turns drinking from the billy after it had cooled enough to handle, and used their fingers to scoop up the noodles. They sat on the foil sheet spread over a layer of dead leaves beneath the tarpaulin Guy had tethered between two large boulders and they basked in the warmth radiating from the roaring fire in front of them.

'Try and get some sleep,' Guy advised. 'We've got another hard day ahead of us tomorrow. I'll keep the fire going as long as I can.'

The padding of two anoraks was enough to make leaning against the smooth rock almost comfortable but, as tired as she was, Jennifer didn't feel inclined to sleep.

'Do you still think you know where we are? What direction we need to go in?'

Guy's grunt was noncommittal. 'Roughly. Whether we can keep to it is another matter. Depends on how many bluffs we need to get past and how dense the forest is. If the weather closes in, we'll be in real trouble.'

Jennifer sat quietly for several minutes. She would have considered herself in real trouble already if it wasn't for Guy. After today she was quite prepared to trust in his leadership, wherever that took them. OK, so he hadn't rushed back to help her when she had fallen on the snow slope, but she had coped, hadn't she?

He hadn't slackened his pace for the rest of the day either, but she had kept up. Trying to prove to Guy that she was capable of more than he thought had pushed her physical boundaries further than she would have imagined possible, and a part of her was feeling pretty damned proud of herself right now.

Guy's movement as he added more wood to the fire drew her attention, and Jennifer knew he wouldn't realise he was being observed from the darkness of the small shelter. She watched as he hunkered down beside the flames and stretched his hands towards the warmth. His physical size alone was enough to give the impression of great strength, but there was something far more solid about this man than mere physical attributes.

The flickering firelight illuminated his features enough for Jennifer to see a repose that was startling. The sadness was only to be expected. How many times that day would Guy's thoughts have returned to Digger? A lot more than hers had, and that had been frequent enough. How much pain had he had to cope with in the past to have reached the level of acceptance he was unknowingly projecting at the moment? And where did anybody gain the strength of character to actually seem at peace in a situation like this?

He belongs here, Jennifer realised suddenly. He was a part of this landscape…the way she had felt for those fleeting moments when watching the sunset on the lake surface. But she didn't feel like that now. She felt left out. And lonely.

'You don't like talking much, do you?'

Guy flicked a brief glance in her direction and then shrugged. 'Is that necessarily a fault? Maybe I'm a good listener.'

She could imagine that to be true. Guy was probably as dependable as a GP as he was proving as a leader in a survival situation. How many people trusted him with their secrets and their health? Even their lives? Jennifer had the strong impression that once you earned loyalty from Dr Knight, you would never lose it. She liked that. It was the kind of dependability her father had always demonstrated. The kind of man Digger must have been.

Guy obviously misinterpreted her sigh. 'Did you have something you wanted to talk *about?*' he asked.

'Not really.' Jennifer chuckled softly. 'I must have bad karma, I guess. I've never been so cut off from the rest of the world and I'm stuck with someone who hates me.'

'I don't hate you. I don't even know you.'

'You think you do. You think I'm useless. Posh. One of a "type" you clearly have no time for.'

'You're rich and famous. Highly successful and very popular. You must be used to living in luxury. It doesn't give us a lot in common, does it?'

'I'm not rich and I'm hardly famous. Outside the world of emergency medicine, I'm a nobody. What's more, I've worked incredibly hard to get where I am and I'm not ashamed of it.'

'I never suggested you should be.'

'Your tone suggested it.'

'All I'm saying is that we're very different people. We may as well live on different planets as far as our daily lives and backgrounds go.'

'What makes you so sure?' Jennifer let her breath out in an exasperated huff. 'For your information, I grew up in the country. On a dairy farm on the outskirts of a one-horse town in Taranaki. My dad was a share-milker and my mum died when I was eight. We had nothing. My dad worked to help me get a better life and I got up at 4:00 a.m. every day so I wouldn't let him down. I helped milk the cows. I worked hard enough at school to get labelled a nerd and had no real friends. I left my dad living alone so I could go to university and med school. He was *proud* of me.'

'I'm sure he was.' Guy added some more sticks to the fire. 'Did you ever want to go back?'

'Of course. I went home to visit Dad as often as I could.' Which hadn't been nearly often enough in recent years. And now it was too late.

'I meant to live.'

'That would have defeated the whole purpose of escaping.'

'And that's what makes us so different.' Guy nodded. 'I wanted to escape as well when *my* mother died. I was eighteen. It was Digger that persuaded me to go to med school and helped me fund it. He knew I'd have to go back one day, even if it did take me ten years to realise how much I hated the city.'

'If you hated it so much, why did it take so long?'

'Med school kept me pretty focussed. And then I had another reason I couldn't leave.'

'Which was?'

'I got married.'

'Oh.' Jennifer blinked in surprise. Of course. Why wouldn't he be married? He probably had his wife and several kids tucked away in a country cottage behind a white picket fence covered in roses. Then she remembered his tone. 'You make it sound like a problem.'

'Turned out that way.' Guy snorted. 'I made the mistake of picking one of your lot.'

'*My* lot?'

'A townie.'

'I just told you I wasn't a townie.' Jennifer could well remember the insult levelled at city dwellers who decided they wanted to join a rural community. A single word, but it spoke volumes about their ignorance and unacceptability.

'You are by inclination. You couldn't wait to escape. You've never gone back.'

Jennifer was silent. There was no argument there. The isolation of rural life held no appeal whatsoever. She didn't want their conversation to end just yet, however. The feeling of companionship was too valuable.

'*You* went back,' she observed quietly. 'What about your wife?'

'She tried it for a while. Said it would kill her if she tried any longer.' Guy's tone was bitter. 'It had already killed her love for me.'

'But not yours for her?' It was an incredibly personal question and Jennifer wouldn't have been surprised if Guy told her to mind her own business. She was quite ready for a rebuke when he finally spoke but, again, he surprised her.

'You can't keep loving someone if it has to be on their planet and the atmosphere's incompatible with your own.' Guy cleared his throat, which came across as a kind of verbal shrug. 'She's happy now. Married to a plastic surgeon and living in Sydney. I believe they've got a holiday house on some Fijian island for when they want a break from the rat race.' Guy started banking up the fire as he spoke. 'It's all ancient history.' He moved back to lean on a boulder and closed his eyes. 'Get some sleep, Jenna. *I* intend to.'

That was the end of the conversation. Sleep wanted to claim Jennifer's exhausted body now, but her brain held on for a few more minutes. No wonder Guy didn't think much of her. It fitted. The impression she'd had earlier that it would take a lot to break this man's loyalty returned. How much stronger would that loyalty be to a woman he loved? One that he had made a commitment to spend the rest of his life with? The pain of having that union destroyed was quite likely great enough to have prevented him ever risking his heart again. Or even trusting a woman, let alone a townie, on a personal basis. She was also aware of a sneaking sympathy for the woman involved in that shared history.

At this point in time she herself might be sharing this man's planet, but he was quite right. The atmosphere was incompatible for long-term survival and she'd be stepping off at the first opportunity. Once she reached safety and civilisation, she doubted that anything would make her want to return.

Ever.

CHAPTER FIVE

'YOU actually do this for *fun?*'

'Yep.'

Jennifer's face twisted into lines of disbelief as she turned to clamber backwards down a narrow channel between two huge boulders. Spray from the small waterfall to her left sent an icy rainfall to splatter her head and she could feel the drops collecting into runnels down the length of her spine.

They had been following the course of this mountain stream for what felt like an eternity. Now deep in the rainforest, the thick canopy prevented any warmth from sunshine and the sound of rushing water had become oppressive white noise that covered any sound with the potential to make this journey a little more tolerable. Like the buzz of a small plane or the chop of an approaching helicopter. Or the gentle cacophony of bird life. Or even conversation.

Guy was at least ten metres in front of Jennifer and he managed to stay at precisely that distance no matter how hard she tried to close the gap. That meant shouting if she wanted to talk to him and Jennifer was far too weary to shout. She needed every ounce of energy she could summon to simply keep moving.

It would be so much easier to be covering the type of terrain that had led to the lake yesterday. Even to be picking their way across snow. But, no, they were making their way slowly down a much harder slope, negotiating boulders, fallen tree trunks and sometimes thick vegetation, which all required a huge physical effort.

Shirley's suede shoes were hopeless. More than once Jennifer had slipped and had had to catch herself to prevent a fall. The firm splinting Guy had provided for her arm couldn't prevent the agony when she had to use that limb to save herself. Her guide didn't seem too bothered by his own injuries. He limped occasionally and she had seen his face set into grimly determined lines at times, but he hadn't slackened his pace or given them a rest yet.

He moved as though he knew exactly where they were going. As though he was actually *enjoying* the challenge.

'It's beyond me.'

'What is?' Guy was slowing down. Finally.

'How anyone could enjoy doing *this*.' Jennifer stepped up on a rock and then found a flat patch of shingle to hop down towards. Her legs protested the effort and she sighed. 'At least I'm getting all the exercise I need for the rest of my life here. I think I'll even start driving to work and that only takes me ten minutes to walk.' Jennifer was about to pass Guy as she spoke, but she didn't stop. It wasn't exactly a difficult route, was it? All they had been doing for hours now had been following this damn stream.

'I wouldn't do that if I were you.'

'What?'

'Look up, Jenna.'

Jennifer raised her gaze from finding the next foothold. 'I don't see anything.'

'Precisely. Where do you think the stream has gone?'

Jennifer took a cautious step forward. The sound of the water had changed as well. The gurgle of a fast, rocky flow had become more distant—a solid roar. She saw why when she stepped high enough to see past the ferns crowding tree trunks on either side of the stream.

She stepped back hurriedly. 'It's a waterfall!' she cried in dismay. 'Down a *cliff!*'

'We'll have to head along the ridge and find another way down.'

'Oh…*great!*'

Jennifer's mutter was inaudible. Once again, Guy was leading the way and this time they were heading into the forest. Uphill. He couldn't know what direction he was going in. They could be doing some vast circle that would lead them back to the lake.

They were completely lost and no rescue team would spot them hidden beneath the canopy of dense rainforest. She couldn't see why Guy was bothering to even mark their route as he bent yet another fern frond, turning the silver side uppermost to shine amongst the dark green foliage.

The trust she had bestowed on this man last night was wearing very thin, his stamina and calm demeanour no longer any comfort. He was an alien species all right. He'd just keep going until he dropped, and he'd probably do that with little or no communication. No wonder his wife had fled back to civilisation. She herself *should* have stayed with the plane. At least she wouldn't have been left feeling so unwanted by the lack of conversation her companions could have offered.

The bitter train of thought led back to Digger, and Jennifer knew she shouldn't judge Guy Knight's personality on his current state. She had to remember he was trying to save them both right now, and as long as they survived she couldn't care less what sort of person he was anyway.

'Take a break, Jenna.' Guy had chosen a fallen moss-covered tree trunk as a resting place.

Jennifer said nothing as she sat down.

'How are the feet holding up?'

'I'm keeping up, aren't I?'

'You're doing well.' Guy nodded.

Jennifer refused to let the praise warm her. 'Have you got any idea where we are right now?'

'Only vaguely. I'm still watching the sun.'

'You can't even *see* the sun.'

'I can see its direction.' Guy pointed and for the first time Jennifer took a real look at the wider area of the forest.

Huge, ancient trees were dotted surprisingly sparsely across a forest floor thick with ferns and smaller, native shrubs. Sunlight filtered through the canopy to give a hazy spotlight effect in which she could see a swarm of tiny insects. A fantail hovered, catching a meal, and between its friendly squeaks Jennifer heard the sound of another bird call.

'That was a bellbird, wasn't it?'

'Sure was.'

'And these are beech trees, right?'

'Yep.'

Jennifer took a deep breath, taking in the unfamiliar scent of a landscape untouched by man—a rich aroma of moisture, earth and the warmth of the sun. It wasn't quiet at all now that she was actually listening. The bird life was everywhere. She could hear the movement of dry twigs and leaves and even the heavy beat of a wood pigeon's large wings. For an instant that sense of belonging came back. The feeling of being part of something extraordinary.

'It *is* beautiful,' she whispered.

'But you wouldn't do it for fun?' Guy was watching her with a curious expression.

'No way.' Jennifer wanted to dismiss both her unsettling response to the setting and the heat that Guy's gaze seemed to generate. 'I'd buy a painting, though.'

He snorted. 'That'd be right. Hang it somewhere to complement the ivory carpets and leather couches. Sit and look at it while you're sipping a glass of Chardonnay.'

'You still think I'm a townie, don't you? Driven by ambition and money and all the shallow values you country hicks associate with city dwellers?' Jennifer was angered by more than the putdown, but she wasn't at all sure why. 'Sure, the scenery's pretty in the wild but you can find just as much ugliness in isolated communities as you can in any city. I've *been* there. I know just how shallow and petty-minded people can be in small towns.' Jennifer stood up. The break wasn't proving exactly restful anymore. 'And what does it say about you, wanting to isolate yourself? Maybe your wife was escaping more than a dead end as far as her social life and any career were going.'

She turned her back on Guy and waited. A long, silent minute passed.

'Are we going, then?' she queried tightly.

Guy got slowly to his feet. 'I thought you were taking the lead here, Dr Allen.'

Jennifer's jaw tightened. A fat lot of good that would do either of them. 'It's actually *Professor* Allen, if you want to get really formal. Or should that be shallow?'

The look she received made Jennifer feel ashamed of her outburst. The way she'd felt after verbally abusing Guy when he had caused the tail section of the plane wreckage to slide when she'd still been trapped inside it. She was far too exhausted to try and analyse why she felt so ashamed of herself. Instead, she looked away.

'Sorry,' she muttered. 'But I'd really like to get out of here.'

'You and me both, babe.' Guy stepped ahead and within a minute they were back in what felt like a familiar routine. Slogging on, with Guy leading the way, marking their route at intervals, pushing a track through heavier undergrowth, watching the sun and changing direction occasionally.

They needed food. And water. When they came across another waterway, Jennifer had no idea whether it was the same stream that had fed the waterfall, and she didn't care. They could quench their thirst and now they had a new track to follow along its banks.

An hour ticked miserably past as she forced her body to keep functioning. And then another. But Jennifer knew she was slowing badly. Had Guy intended to stop for a rest or was he watching for her? It was getting harder each time she put one foot in front of the other and Guy looked just as close to the end of his tether.

'Sorry.' It was the first time Jennifer had spoken since her last apology but she didn't notice she was repeating herself. 'I am *trying* to keep up.'

'You're doing OK.'

'It's getting darker, isn't it?'

'We'll have to stop soon and build a shelter.' Guy closed his eyes wearily. 'Another day should do it. I'm pretty sure we're going in the right direction.'

'Well, somebody's been here before anyway.'

Dark eyes snapped open. 'What makes you say that?'

'There was a bit of metal nailed to a tree. Is that to mark possum traps or something?'

'Where was it?' Guy was on his feet again now, staring intently at Jennifer.

'Back a bit. I can't remember how far.'

'Stay there.' And Guy was gone, striding back the way they'd come with a barely noticeable limp.

Jennifer sat and waited. She heard twigs crack as Guy headed back and then the sounds faded again. Long minutes passed and Jennifer could feel a curious lethargy taking over as sleep started a seductive pull.

Suddenly she found her upper arms being gripped. She was pulled to her feet and Guy was leaning down. Planting a firm kiss on her lips.

'You've done it, babe,' he said softly. 'You've found a track. I found the marker and the next one and I think I know exactly where we are.'

'Really?' His excitement was contagious. Or was it the effect of that kiss? Jennifer's smile felt strange. Rusty. 'You mean we're nearly out of here?'

'I think there's a hut maybe two or three kilometres away. If I'm right, it'll have a stove and a radio. Can you make it?'

'You bet.' Jennifer stumbled in her eagerness to follow.

'Take it easy,' Guy cautioned. 'And be careful. You don't want to break an ankle now.'

He showed her how the small triangle of metal pointed in the direction they needed to take. They found another one ten minutes later, and Jennifer could feel a welcome surge of renewed hope. And energy. Safety beckoned. They were almost there.

'We have to cross this stream.' Guy was scanning what seemed more like a small river. The light was definitely fading now but Jennifer could still make out the pale gleam of a piece of metal on the far bank.

'There's the marker!' She stepped forward, her foot sinking into several inches of icy water.

'Wait! This isn't the best place to cross.'

'But the marker's right there. We have to cross here.'

'It's too fast. That centre point is deeper than it looks.'

'It wouldn't even come to my knees.'

'There may be a hole we can't see in this light. Or underwater snags. The current would be enough to knock you off your feet and you don't want to get swept away among boulders.'

'But—'

'Just shut up a minute,' Guy ordered. 'And let me think.'

The longer he waited, the darker it was going to get. If they left it too long, they wouldn't be able to find further markers on the other side and they would be doomed to spend another night in the open, instead of reaching a hut where they would find shelter and warmth. Possibly even food and the promise of imminent rescue.

Jennifer took another step. The water was only ankle deep for the most part, for heaven's sake. The bottom had small stones that provided reasonably firm footing and there were larger boulders as anchor points if she needed them.

'We're wasting time,' she informed Guy. 'I can do this. Just watch.'

She almost made it. Even in the knee-deep water she was able to stand up against the current. But then a branch came downstream, went between her legs, caught on a rock and twisted sideways. Jennifer was felled instantly.

Immersion in the icy water was enough of a shock to make her gasp, and her mouth filled with water she couldn't prevent herself from inhaling. She couldn't cough. Couldn't breathe. She was being swept downstream like the branch, about to hit her head on a boulder and drown, but it was all happening so fast there was no time for terror.

Her rescue seemed to happen just as fast. Guy had entered the water downstream. He caught Jennifer and hauled her to her feet, then half pulled, half carried her towards the shore. She sank to her knees when he released her. She coughed, spluttered and then burst into tears. The terror caught up with her then. And the mind-numbing chill of being soaked in water that wasn't far above freezing level.

'Come on.' Guy clearly wasn't going to waste any more time. 'You're alive. You've got to keep moving until we get to the hut.'

'I can't.' Jennifer huddled, her arms wrapped around her legs. 'I c-can't m-move.' The shivering was so violent it was painful.

Guy muttered what had to be something Jennifer wouldn't have wanted to hear anyway. He pulled her roughly to her feet and then bent to put an arm behind her knees.

'Hang on,' he instructed grimly.

Jennifer wrapped stiff arms around his neck and held on, even though she knew the splint on her arm must be cutting into his shoulder. She could feel the jerk of unsteady movement as he negotiated the track and adjusted to his burden. She could feel the limp that became progressively more pronounced, but she could do nothing more than hang on. And pray.

Her awareness of anything more than the sound of Guy's rasping breaths, the pounding of his heart and the tight grip of his arms faded. Jennifer had no idea how long he carried her like that. A distant memory nagged until she caught it. The day her mother had died. The bewilderment and pain. The solid feel of her father's arms and the sound of his voice trying to create an anchor in a child's shattered life. She could even hear the rumble of his deep voice.

'It's OK, Jenna. I've got you. We'll get through this together, you and me.'

It was a shock to open her eyes at the jolt of being lowered to the ground and to see Guy's face instead of her father's. Had *he* spoken those words? No. Jennifer shook her head to try and orient herself.

'We've made it.' Guy's voice sounded ragged. 'We're safe, Jenna. Look.'

The hut sat in a small clearing, a large, dark shape against an even darker background.

'It's the Welcome Flat hut,' Guy told her. 'A mansion compared to most tramping huts, and the only two-storied one that I know of. It's years since I've been here, but it should have a coal stove and a radio.'

Jennifer stared at the solid wooden door. 'What if…it's locked?'

'Huts are never locked.' Guy led the way and turned the handle. 'See?'

Not only was the hut open, it had been left immaculately tidy by the last people to use it. Fuel for the stove was abundant and in what seemed like no time at all the light from the flames revealed other treasures. Like a hurricane lamp that created enough light for them to see the supply of canned and dried food left in case of emergencies and a radio. Guy seemed to have no problem in turning it on and changing frequency while searching for a response.

'Welcome Flat Hut,' he said repeatedly. 'This is Guy Knight requesting assistance. Is anybody receiving?'

Then, miraculously, a response came.

'Department of Conservation base station here. Are you from the plane that went down two days ago?'

'Affirmative.'

'How many of you are there?'

'Two.'

'Are you injured?'

'Not badly. We've walked out from the crash site.'

Jennifer huddled near the stove but the warmth didn't seem able to penetrate her layers of wet clothing. She had stopped shivering and felt incredibly drowsy, but if she was entering a more advanced state of hypothermia she couldn't have cared less. She listened to the discussion of whether to send a search-and-rescue team in to meet them at first light or a helicopter to evacuate them.

Apparently it was a six-hour tramp to where vehicles could access the track from the main highway at the Karangarua River. Guy didn't seem to think Jennifer was able to do the walk, and she wasn't going to argue.

She didn't even protest when Guy came over and ordered her to take off all her clothes. Her fingers refused to cooperate, however, so she stood there like a statue while Guy pulled soggy garments from her one by one. He left her bra and knickers on but she was past caring.

Having draped the clothes over a chair close to the heat of the stove, Guy took off his leather jacket and hung it over Jennifer's shoulders. Then he astonished her by picking her up in his arms again.

'Come on,' he said. 'I know how to warm you up.'

Was he going to take her to lie on one of the bunk mattresses with him? Skin to skin, as the common lore regarding treatment of hypothermia suggested was best?

He'd already kissed her. He'd stripped off her clothes.
The thought of further intimacy didn't bother Jennifer.
Nothing bothered her. Even being taken outside into the
cold night air.

'Wait a minute!' The words were spoken aloud as the
chill bit into her exposed skin. She tried to move but the
grasp of Guy's arms was way too firm. 'What the hell
do you think you're doing?'

They had finally reached safety. Warmth. Even in her
fuzzy mental state Jennifer knew she needed warmth
above anything else.

'Don't argue,' Guy ordered brusquely. 'Trust me.'

She had done precisely that for two days now.
Another few minutes probably couldn't hurt, and it
seemed far less time than that when Guy stopped and
put her gently onto her feet.

'Hot pools,' he said. 'As good as a bath, I promise.'

He was pulling off his own clothes as he spoke, and
Jennifer stared. Maybe it was the relief of being still
being alive after such a harrowing experience or maybe
her brain had ceased to function in any normal fashion,
but Guy suddenly seemed the most desirable man
Jennifer had ever seen in her life.

He stripped down to boxer shorts and Jennifer wasn't
surprised to see the lines of hard muscle without a trace
of fat on him anywhere. Then he dropped the shorts and
Jennifer felt a hot wash of acute embarrassment. Not that
Guy seemed to share it. He slid the jacket from her
shoulders.

'You may as well leave your undies on,' he said
calmly. 'They're soaked anyway. You can take them off
when we're back at the hut.'

He led her into one of several steaming pools and held
her when her legs wobbled. He found a spot that allowed

him to sit and hold her with the water level up to their
necks.

'Don't let any of the water get up your nose,' he
warned. 'New Zealand's hot pools are notorious for
causing amoebic meningitis.'

They stayed there long enough for the warmth to
reach Jennifer's core and for her brain to start taking a
more active interest in her surroundings again.

Too active. She was sitting almost in a naked man's
lap. A man who was a loner by choice and despised the
type of person he thought she was, but a physically extremely attractive man. Someone who had, undoubtedly,
saved her life. More than once.

The force of the gratitude she had no way of ade-
quately conveying stayed with Jennifer as they made
their way back to the hut. She stayed by the stove, wearing Guy's leather jacket and nothing else while she
waited for her clothing to dry and the baked beans and
tinned casserole Guy was heating to be ready to eat.

The warmth from burning coal soon heated the whole
interior of the small building but neither of them wanted
to move far from the source of the heat. Guy put mattresses from the bunks on the floor and they sat there to
eat.

'Feeling warmer?'

'Yes, thanks.' Jennifer tugged at the jacket, which was
long enough to cover her decently but still left a rather
long length of thigh exposed. 'I'll be glad when my
clothes are dry.'

'They'll take a while yet. I'll make us a cup of tea.
Do you mind having it black?'

'Hardly.' Jennifer's smile was wry. 'I'm not sure that
I'll ever take having milk in hot drinks for granted ever
again. Or even having hot drinks.'

'There's a lot of things you might not take for granted,' Guy agreed quietly.

Jennifer nodded, her gaze catching his. 'Like being alive,' she murmured. 'I have you to thank for that, Guy.'

'You managed it by yourself,' he countered.

'I wouldn't have without you pushing me. If I hadn't been trying to prove I wasn't some useless, soft townie, I would have given up before I even climbed onto that snow slope.'

'You never know what you're capable of until you really try. You're not soft, Jenna. Not by a long shot. And you're certainly not useless.'

'I felt useless,' Jenna whispered. 'Waiting for Digger to die.'

Guy closed his eyes and Jennifer winced at having caused him pain. She reached out and touched his face, offering a touch instead of words because she knew that she could never find the right ones to convey the turmoil of emotions hanging between them.

He seemed to understand. He caught her hand and held it against the roughness of stubble on his cheek. Then he turned his head and she felt the contrast of the softness of lips as he pressed them against her palm.

Jennifer's quick intake of breath made him glance up and catch her gaze again, and that was a big mistake.

She looked like a child. Huge, blue, vulnerable eyes. All the pain of loss, the determination to survive and the gratitude for his assistance were stamped clearly in the blue depths, and for a moment Guy was lost. It was an automatic gesture to take her into his arms, but he was running on more than instinct as he responded to her upturned face and covered her lips with his own. And suddenly making love seemed the only thing they could possibly do. An affirmation of life, maybe, that only they could share.

They had been through too much together to be considered strangers, but they would probably never see each other again when this was over and that didn't matter. With every touch they were confirming that something good still existed despite loss. That the effort to survive had been worthwhile.

Jennifer seemed as hungry for the physical release as Guy certainly was. They had a pocket of time in which they were still isolated from reality, and Jennifer exceeded the qualities of any partner Guy might have conjured up to provide a fantasy. Pale, soft skin felt like silk beneath his hands. Surprisingly full breasts tasted like honey and the faint musky scent of her arousal drew him irresistibly closer.

He wanted Jennifer more than he had ever wanted any woman, and yet he was able to go more slowly than he ever had before. To take care not to hurt her arm or her feet. To touch and taste and linger in wonderment at how poignant the sharp sensation of desire could be. And she was as generous a lover as he could have wished for.

She returned every touch and answered every incoherent murmur. She took over the lead every time he paused so that it became a kind of dance. A courtship ritual that would never lead beyond brief fulfilment— but that simply didn't register as significant because they had just spent so many hours together taking each moment as it came.

And when this moment came, it was blinding in its satisfaction. Guy had never experienced anything remotely comparable. The release for them both seemed to exhaust any last possible reserves of energy and, entangled in each other's limbs, they finally slept.

CHAPTER SIX

A HELICOPTER had certainly been the best choice.

The sound of the approaching aircraft was enough to wake both Guy and Jennifer from an almost comatose state of exhaustion. Any awkwardness at finding themselves still naked and closely intertwined beneath an old woollen blanket and a layer of clothing evaporated the instant they both tried to move.

The groans were simultaneous but the pain was enough to freeze Jennifer, whereas Guy managed to roll over and sit up. He picked up items of Jennifer's clothing, which were now dry.

'You might like to put something on,' he said drily. 'We're going to have company any minute.'

Jennifer tried again. She twisted away from Guy and used her right arm to lever herself into a sitting position. The pain and effort required were unbelievable. How on earth had they managed to make love only hours ago? Jennifer couldn't even remember her broken arm having been any kind of obstacle. In fact, when she remembered just how active they had been at times, a flush of deep embarrassment washed up to heat her face.

It wouldn't be so bad if Guy had said something to at least acknowledge what had happened. Or ask how she was feeling. He didn't even make personal communication in the form of eye contact, however, and by now he was half-dressed and Jennifer was still totally exposed in her nakedness. The engine noise of the helicopter was deafening. It seemed to be hovering directly over the roof of the hut.

'They'll probably be able to land near the hot pools,' Guy said. 'That'll save having to winch us up.'

Winching up her own bra was clearly an impossibility because of her arm, but Jennifer dismissed any idea of asking Guy for assistance as soon as the thought occurred. He was far too concerned with getting himself respectable for greeting a rescue team, and Jennifer was now aware of the same vibes she'd had about following him away from the crash site in the aftermath of Digger's death.

She was an unwanted liability. Guy had an agenda and he would far rather follow it alone.

The woollen top was manageable—just—but her skirt was still hanging over the chair. Jennifer tried to move again.

'I can't stand up,' she said in dismay. 'My feet feel like they're full of broken glass.'

They had swollen again, far more than they had after the first day's walking. Guy's ankle wasn't looking pretty either. He abandoned his attempt to fit a sock over badly discoloured and misshapen flesh, gave Jennifer a brief glance and then pulled her skirt off the chair and threw it to her just as the door of the hut opened.

'Hi, there!' The cheerful voice belonged to a small helmeted female. 'How's it going?'

'Maggie!' The smile on Guy's face was warmer than Jennifer would have believed he was capable of, and she experienced a completely bizarre flash of sheer jealousy. 'I wasn't expecting you!'

'I wasn't expecting me either.' The paramedic was unbuckling the top of a kit that looked like a tramper's pack. 'I had to get up at the crack of dawn for this. You owe me, Guy.'

'Sorry.'

'Actually...' Maggie was smiling at Jennifer as she spoke '...we were all up anyway. The search-and-rescue effort to find you guys has had a lot of people losing sleep.' She turned her gaze back to Guy and her smile faded. 'Thank God you're OK,' she said quietly. 'I heard the others weren't so lucky.'

'No.' There was a moment's silence before Guy cleared his throat. 'This is Jennifer Allen, Maggie. She's an emergency consultant. She's got a fractured arm and her feet are a mess, but otherwise she's OK. I imagine she could use some pain relief, though. She isn't able to weight bear anymore.'

'Hi, Jennifer.' The smile was engaging enough for Jennifer to forget that flash of jealousy. 'I'm Maggie Patterson and I'm a paramedic. You'll meet my husband, Hugh, when you get to our ED at Lakeside Hospital.' She pulled a blood-pressure cuff and stethoscope from her kit. 'Can I check you out and get you comfortable before we head off? We'll get you out first, seeing that Guy's in better shape.'

Jennifer smiled back. So Maggie was married, was she? To someone called Hugh? 'Sounds great,' she said.

Now that their rescue was actually in progress and the ordeal almost over, Jennifer's reserves of strength and independence seemed to simply desert her. For once in her life she was happy to give herself up to being cared for by others. The last few days had provided the most extraordinary experiences she was ever likely to have— and that included last night's lovemaking with Guy Knight—but already they were taking on a dream-like quality and the relief to be leaving it all behind was overwhelming.

'Sharp scratch now,' Maggie warned. 'Guy, be a honey and draw up that morphine for me, would you? We'll give her some metaclopramide as well. I don't want my patient getting airsick.'

The drug hit Jennifer like a slug of pure alcohol. Her head swam and the pain in her battered body began to recede.

'This might make you pretty drowsy,' she heard Maggie say. 'I've given you a decent dose. You just try and relax and we'll have you out of here in no time.'

Relaxation had been anathema to Jennifer for virtually her entire life. Spare time was wasted time, and if anyone had told her she would spend over forty-eight hours doing little more than sleeping, she would have shaken her head and smiled at the absurdity of the notion. To find herself awake and content to do nothing more than gaze at the view from her window was equally novel.

Mind you, the view was unparalleled. What other hospital on earth could offer patients this glorious panorama of craggy, snow-topped mountains? The alpine resort of Queenstown nestled at the edge of Wakatipu—a huge and mysterious, glacier-gouged lake at the foot of the Remarkables. Jennifer's close brush with the realities of the rugged landscape in this part of South Island only increased her appreciation of her homeland, and this particular area was a jewel.

Not that she'd want to live here, of course, but it was a great place to visit, and thank goodness some people didn't want to live anywhere else. The medical care she'd received at the gentle but highly competent hands of both Maggie and Hugh Patterson had been as good as she could have wished for in her own large department. Better, even, thanks to the caring staff who had both the time and inclination to become personally involved with their patients.

The district hospital wasn't that isolated either, judging by the number of reporters who had flocked in as news of the survival of plane-crash victims became the story of the week. The first television film crew had been waiting when the helicopter had landed but Jennifer had been barely aware of their presence. She had spoken to several people since, however. Drowsy conversations snatched between long intervals of deep slumber, but they had been enough to provide news footage for television and front-page coverage in every major newspaper in the country.

Several of those newspapers lay discarded on the end of her bed, but Jennifer had no desire to scan them again. The sight of her photographs and reading her quotes had left her vaguely embarrassed. Why hadn't Guy allowed *his* picture to be taken? Or given more than a terse comment about it being 'No big deal. He'd only done what had to be done and they'd been bloody lucky.'

The impression that Jennifer was whingeing about how much of an ordeal it had been or that she was claiming the spotlight to further a personal profile was unavoidable and rather disturbing. It highlighted the vast difference between herself and Guy. He was a loner. A man of the mountains. She hated the absence of crowds and a hectic lifestyle. Her own life was calling her, signalling the end of this interlude of rest and recuperation.

Jennifer sat up. It was early evening, judging by the play of twilight on the mountain peaks outside. Not too late to get herself up and start moving enough to iron out the residual stiffness in her limbs.

Personal items had been brought here from the hotel in which the conference had been held, and Jennifer chose casual woollen trousers and a silk shirt, leaving one sleeve unbuttoned to accommodate the cast on her left arm. Stroking the soft warmth of the bright red Merino sweater she had purchased in the hotel boutique the day she'd arrived, Jennifer decided the hospital's central heating system made it unnecessary. She certainly wasn't intending to set foot outside.

It was, in fact, far more of an effort than she'd anticipated to simply get any distance along the corridor. Jennifer almost regretted not using the set of crutches the physiotherapist had left in her room. Her feet felt like wooden blocks with something unpleasantly sharp coating the soles. She would never have lasted even one more day out in the bush. Guy was right. They *had* been incredibly lucky.

Jennifer sank down onto the cushions of a small couch that marked the bend in the corridor leading to the main staircase. A nurse came out of a nearby room and paused, having spotted her.

'You're up, Jennifer! Are you all right?'

'I'm fine, thanks, Sue. Thought I'd better test out my feet.'

'You might be better to use those crutches to start with. Shall I get them for you?'

'I'll just have a rest for a bit. If I don't make it back to my room, I'll yell for help.'

'Make sure you do.' Sue's smile acknowledged the unlikelihood of someone like Jennifer yelling for help. She walked away, passing the single rooms that led to the main ward. Guy had to be in one of those rooms, and at some point Jennifer would have to visit him to say goodbye. To thank him for saving her life.

But he hadn't been in to see her and the embarrassment factor was becoming increasingly hard to overcome. What could she say? 'Thanks for saving me, Guy, and, oh, yeah, thanks for the sex. It was great.'

Jennifer's soft snort was more for the unsuitability of the adjective than imagining its delivery. 'Great' didn't touch the impact of that experience. It had been incomparable. Jennifer had never been touched quite like that—either physically or emotionally. The place in her soul that had been touched still felt raw, in fact, and Jennifer shied away from prodding it. Her smile was wry. Maybe she should make sure she was at the point of total collapse, having survived a life-threatening situation, before she went to bed with anyone else.

The thought was distasteful enough to be disturbing. Even more disturbing was the conviction that having experienced that extraordinary night with Guy she would never find anyone who had a hope of delivering anything remotely similar.

Guy Knight. Or should that be Night? Any visions of a medieval warrior riding to her rescue were easily replaced by the picture of that lean body, with flickering dim light playing over fluid muscles as it moved over hers.

Jennifer closed her eyes with a silent groan. No. There was no way she could just pop in to visit Guy for a casual farewell. But she couldn't just leave without seeing him, could she? Why the hell hadn't *he* taken the initiative and broken that barrier? Because he was also embarrassed? Because he wished it hadn't happened? Because it wasn't actually worth acknowledging as far as he was concerned?

Fingers of shame clutched at something deep and Jennifer snapped her eyes open to distract herself. She watched a couple of elderly women pause as they reached the top of the stairwell.

'It's tomorrow, isn't it?' one of them said.

'The funeral? Yes.' Her companion paused to unbutton a woollen coat. 'My, it's warm in here, isn't it?'

'So sad.' The first woman rearranged her hold on a large handbag and a bunch of flowers. 'He was the only real father that poor boy ever had.'

Jennifer's interest quickened despite herself. So they were talking about Digger rather than Bill and Shirley. She would like to go to the funeral herself, but maybe it wasn't appropriate. Not if Guy didn't even want to talk to her.

'He's got no one now. No family.'

The woman holding the flowers sniffed audibly. 'That isn't a great loss if you remember his mother.'

The judgmental tone triggered something like anger in Jennifer. Memories of the kind of interference and gossip that were part of the fabric of a small community and one of the things she had been happy to escape. What had been so wrong with Guy's mother? She'd been the woman Digger had loved, hadn't she? Diana. 'The goddess,' he'd called her.

The women were moving towards Jennifer now so, despite their lowered voices, she could still overhear their conversation.

'Such a shame he hasn't married again. If anyone needs a family, that young man does.'

'Well, he didn't choose very wisely, did he? There's plenty of nice local girls who would jump at the chance.'

Jennifer was given a curious glance and one of the women smiled, but neither said anything to her. They were still absorbed in their own interchange.

'Maybe he's too like his mother.' The words faded as

the women headed for what was presumably Guy's room down the corridor. 'He wants what he can't have.'

The arrival of the two women seemed to have prompted an earlier group to finish their visit. Four middle-aged men and women came out of the room. Had Guy been having an endless stream of well-wishers? Had that prevented him from finding the time to visit her perhaps? More likely, being enfolded into the concern of his community had highlighted how different she was. She didn't fit into his life and never would, so breaking any bond they had formed in their time together was inevitable. The timing of that break should not be of any great significance.

This group also paused near the stairwell as they put on extra clothing before heading out into the chill of an early October evening.

'Was that her?' someone asked in a stage whisper. 'That hot-shot professor from Auckland?'

'Yes. I recognise her from the papers.'

'I hear it was her fault the flight plan wasn't logged,' a man said.

'Yeah. Apparently Digger would have been OK if they'd found him a bit quicker.'

Jennifer gritted her teeth. Going to the funeral was definitely not a good idea. Did Guy blame her as well? Was *that* why he was ignoring her?

'She reminds me of someone.' One of the women was pulling a woollen hat over her short brown hair.

'Yeah,' her partner agreed. 'Shannon.'

Who was Shannon? Jennifer wondered. The woman he'd married? Had Guy made love to her because she reminded him of his *ex-wife?* Embarrassment could turn into anger with surprising ease. Jennifer felt used. A snatch of the previous conversation she'd overheard returned. Guy was too like his mother. He wanted what he couldn't have. His ex-wife, maybe.

'Not really to look at.' The group was finally moving away, thank goodness, but their voices floated up the stairwell to Jennifer's now straining ears. 'Though I suppose they're both blonde.'

'More a type,' someone else suggested.

'Yeah.' The male voice sounded appreciative. 'Flashy.'

'Let's just hope Guy didn't fall for *her*.' The faint female voice still managed to sound distinctly possessive.

Someone else clearly agreed. 'We can do without that kind of trouble again.'

Jennifer struggled to her feet. No worries, she was tempted to shout after the group. She had no intention of trying to get any kind of foothold in Guy Knight's life. He was welcome to his mountains and his protective, insular and probably ignorant community.

Jennifer couldn't wait to get away.

Back to her real life. And the sooner the better.

'Are you sure about this?' Hugh Patterson was frowning. 'You're still going to need a lot of rest. I don't want you trying to get back to work for at least a week. Preferably ten days.'

'I'll be far happier when I get home,' Jennifer assured the doctor. 'I'll rest, I promise. And I won't try going back to work too soon.'

'Too soon' was a nicely elastic term. Jennifer had every intention of getting back into a familiar routine as soon as she possibly could. She could get a lightweight cast put on her arm in a day or two and she should be able to function in some kind of useful capacity after that.

'OK, then.' Huge was smiling. 'I'll sort out the discharge paperwork first thing in the morning. When would you like a flight booked?'

'What's the first flight out tomorrow?'

Hugh shook his head but he was still smiling. 'Maybe I'd better do that paperwork before I go home tonight.'

'Thanks. I'd appreciate that.'

'Don't sneak off without saying goodbye, will you? Maggie would love to see you as well. She's based in the ambulance station right next door.'

'I'll make sure I pop in and thank her. She was terrific.'

'She is, isn't she?' Hugh's quiet pride had the effect of making Jennifer feel even more isolated than her current location dictated.

She needed to escape. To reassure herself that she was still the same person she had been before she'd come here. A successful, respected and popular person.

Someone who mattered.

Sneaking off would have been a highly desirable course of action as far as avoiding Guy was concerned, but Jennifer would not allow herself to take the easy way out. Her flight was due to leave at 10:00 a.m. but the airport was very close to the hospital. Maggie had come in to say goodbye already so Jennifer left it till 9:30 a.m. to go to Guy's room.

She was surprised to see an IV line attached to his arm and a cast on the foot raised on pillows. So the ankle had been fractured after all. How on earth had he managed that walk? She was also taken aback to see how pale Guy looked. The colour of his skin made those dark eyes stand out, and Jennifer suddenly wished she hadn't screwed up the courage to make this visit. She felt like a bug trapped in a tiny jar under scrutiny to determine her species.

'They said you were doing fine,' she said uncomfortably. 'You don't *look* fine.'

'I got a bit of an infection in that cut on my leg. Hence the antibiotics.' Guy tweaked the plastic line snaking from his arm. 'This is coming out this morning. They'll patch up the window in my cast and then I'll be off.'

Off to Digger's funeral probably.

'I'm heading away myself.' Jennifer dropped her gaze. The shame she felt now had nothing to do with the physical intimacy that had ended her time with this man. He'd been in far worse shape than she had realised, and she hadn't even bothered getting down the corridor to see him. 'I just wanted to come and…and thank you.'

'You're very welcome,' Guy said politely.

'I don't really know what to say,' Jennifer admitted. 'You saved my life and I'm never going to forget that.'

She met his gaze again. It wasn't just her survival she wasn't going to forget. Not by a long shot. Should she say something about that night? Was *he* going to say something? She couldn't look away. The understanding of what was unspoken was there quite clearly.

'So it's back to reality, then?' Guy's voice was very soft.

She nodded, unable to find any words. Their night together hadn't been 'real' but then, she already knew that, didn't she?

'The nightmare's over.' Guy nodded as he broke the eye contact. 'Almost over anyway. I've got a funeral to go to this afternoon.'

'I know. I wanted to go but then I thought I wouldn't be very welcome.'

'Why not?' The tone was disinterested.

'I think people blame me for what happened. I mean the change of route that meant we weren't found quickly.' Jennifer bit her lip. If anyone had reason to feel bitter towards her, it had to be Guy. He'd lost the closest thing he had to a family member, hadn't he? 'I wish I could have done more,' she ploughed on miserably. 'I'm really so sorry about Digger.'

'Yeah.' The look Jennifer received was closed off enough to appear blank. 'Forget it, Jenna. It's over. And it wasn't your fault.'

He closed his eyes and Jennifer glanced at her watch. 'I'd better go. I hope you get well soon.' She backed towards the door. 'Thanks again, Guy…for everything. I'll keep in touch.'

Guy didn't open his eyes. 'Sure. Me, too.'

But they wouldn't. Jennifer knew that with absolute certainty as the wheels of her plane lifted from the tarmac and the aircraft pulled up into a sharp ascent to gain the height needed to leave the mountainous terrain.

Maybe she would never forget but if she didn't distance herself, the memories would haunt her far too deeply. Staying in touch with Guy would only prolong trying to move on from a shattering experience, to put it into a perspective that wouldn't interfere with her future.

Guy would feel exactly the same way. He was, no doubt, breathing a deep sigh of relief right now as he heard the plane circle above the hospital. Maybe he was even watching from a veranda, his relief evident in a wry smile.

She was an alien and she was returning to her own planet.

CHAPTER SEVEN

THE man looked far too fit to be sitting in an emergency department.

His tanned, lean chest had just a faint cover of dark hair in a V that pointed to an admirably flat belly.

Professor Jennifer Allen had yet another one of those momentary lapses, but it was easy enough to recover this time. Guy's shoulders had been much broader and this man was on the skinny side of lean. His ribs were prominent rather than overlaid with a firm layer of muscle.

It was ridiculous to be still experiencing these lapses anyway. Despite the intensity of their time together, Guy was still a stranger. She would never see him again so it was high time she stopped thinking about him so often.

Missing him.

The house surgeon was giving Jennifer a curious look so she smiled reassuringly, introduced herself to the patient and then caught the young doctor's eye again.

'This is Peter Cowl,' she was informed. 'He's twenty-six and has a history of spontaneous pneumothorax. He came in with sudden onset, unilateral, localised chest pain and shortness of breath.'

The patient did not appear to be in a state of respiratory distress that might indicate the development of a tension pneumothorax. 'What's the oxygen saturation?'

'He came in at 86. It's gone up to 92 on high-flow oxygen.'

'How are you feeling, Peter?'

'Bit puffed. Not too bad.'

'How many times has this happened before?'

'Three or four.'

'Have you needed aspiration with a needle or tube before?'

'Twice.' The young man grimaced. 'Would prefer not to…do it again.'

'Sure. We'll keep an eye on you and run a few tests, then we'll decide how we're going to manage this.' Jennifer turned back to the house surgeon. 'Get chest X-rays, both inspiratory and expiratory. And we'll need an arterial blood-gas sample. Have you done one of those yet?' She smiled again at the nervous head shake. 'Get one of the registrars to assist you, then. I'll help if I can, but it's a bit busy out there.'

Jennifer was already moving away from the cubicle. Busy was the kind of understatement that made light of their workload—a coping mechanism. The emergency department of Auckland Central was currently stretched to its limit. It would fit right into Jennifer's day if Peter Cowl did develop a tension pneumothorax that required urgent decompression—probably when she was tied up with another critical intervention.

At least there were a dozen or so other people somewhere in this department qualified to perform such a procedure, plus all the equipment and backup they could possibly need. None of these doctors were ever likely to have to try and manage an emergency perched on top of a mountain in a makeshift tent, with only limited gear and no hope of assistance. Or success, in the long run. They had no idea how spoilt they all were.

'Dr Allen, can you spare a minute?'

'What is it, Doug?' The registrar was competent enough for his anxious expression to ring an alarm bell.

'I've got a sixty-nine year old chap with sepsis from

a urinary tract infection. He's as flat as a pancake and I can't get any peripheral IV access. He needs fluid resus, stat, and it's going to take too long to do a surgical cutdown.'

'Try a central venous line, then.' Jennifer caught the message in the glance she received, and remembered that Doug had had major difficulties the last time he'd tried the procedure, but if this patient was in septic shock, this was hardly the best situation for a teaching session.

'Are you set up?'

'Yes.'

'OK, I'm all yours.'

'Are you sure?' Doug eyed the cast on her arm but Jennifer nodded decisively.

'It's not a problem anymore. See?' She waggled her fingers at him. 'I've got full mobility in my hand.'

Doug led the way towards one of the curtained resuscitation areas past the central desk.

'MVA coming in,' the triage nurse warned Jennifer. 'Three patients. Two status 1. ETA five minutes.'

'Is the trauma room clear?'

'Just.'

'Get the team together. John or Adam can lead if they're free. I'll be tied up for a few minutes.'

A woman with a shrieking toddler in her arms stepped out of their way, but Jennifer had to swerve to avoid a bed being rapidly manoeuvred.

'Sorry, Prof,' the orderly called.

'Not a problem, Deane. I'm just as bad with supermarket trollies!'

The patient with the UTI was looking extremely unwell. Doug rapidly gave her the information that added up to a shocked condition. Colin Smith was febrile, hypotensive, tachycardic and confused. He had a forty-eight-hour history of urinary frequency and pain, had been to his GP that morning, having passed blood, but hadn't filled his prescription for antibiotics yet.

'It was grandparents' day at Alice's kindy,' his wife explained to Jennifer. 'He said he was fine and he'd start the pills later, but then he just got so sick so quickly. He started vomiting then so there didn't seem much point in trying to get him to swallow pills.'

Colin had tufty grey hair rather like Digger's had been. Jennifer could just imagine him toughing it out and pretending he was fine. She picked up his hand, noting the cool, clammy feel of his skin.

'Colin? Can you open your eyes?' She smiled at him when he complied. 'Hi, there. I'm Dr Allen, one of the consultants here.'

'You'd better watch out.' Her patient managed to return her smile. 'My wife might see you holding my hand.'

'Do you know where you are, Colin?'

'Heaven,' he murmured. 'Are you the boss angel?'

'We need to get an intravenous line into you to treat your infection,' Jennifer told him. 'And your veins aren't cooperating so I'm going to put one in just under your collarbone. Are you happy for me to do that?'

'You do whatever you like, love. I'm just…' The words trailed off into an incoherent mumble and he closed his eyes again.

Mrs Smith pressed her hand to her mouth. 'He's really sick, isn't he?'

'You hold his hand,' Jennifer encouraged. 'And we'll get on with getting him better.' She plucked a mask from the wall dispenser. 'Let's have a head-down tilt, Doug. Is there some local drawn up on that trolley?'

'I'll get it.' An assisting nurse was holding a gown

out for Jennifer. Another nurse was preparing to swab
Colin's chest for the sterile procedure.

'Thanks.' Jennifer turned to get the ties on her gown
attended to. 'I'll need one large glove to get over this
cast.'

Seconds later, they were ready. With the skin well
infiltrated with local anaesthetic, Jennifer picked up a
10-gauge cannula.

'Turn his head for me, Doug, and keep things nice
and still.' Feeling along the clavicle, Jennifer chose the
point of entry and was pleased to find an instant flash-
back. She withdrew the needle, leaving the plastic cannula in place. 'OK. I'm ready for the guide wire.'

The flexible wire was passed into the vein and then a
catheter introduced over the wire. Jennifer watched the
screen of the monitor as she threaded the guide wire,
making sure the wire didn't travel far enough to irritate
the heart and cause a rhythm disturbance.

Now that access had been established, the rest of this
procedure was straightforward. The catheter would be
stitched into place and covered with a dressing. A chest
X-ray would confirm its correct positioning and blood
samples could be drawn before fluids and drugs were
administered.

'Do you want me to take over?' Doug asked.

'I'm fine for a minute or two.' Jennifer reached for
the suture needle. 'You're doing really well, Colin.
We're almost done.'

The relief on Mrs Smith's face was patent, but she
still held her husband's hand tightly. 'You're going to
be fine, love. Alice is going to come in to see you later.
She's drawing you a special picture.'

'How old is Alice?' Jennifer queried.

'She's four. Her little brother's two. We've got six grandchildren now…and they all adore their grandad.'

'I'm sure.' Jennifer smiled as she tied off the last knot. 'Do they get lots of time with him?'

'Now that he's finally retired, they do. It was hard to get him away from work, though.'

'I'm not retired,' Colin mumbled as they raised his head position. 'I've just cut down my hours a bit.'

'What do you do?' Doug's eyebrows had been rising steadily during the conversation, but Jennifer ignored his surprise. Why shouldn't she take the time to get to know her patients a little better?

'I'm a vet,' Colin told her. 'Small animal practice.'

'He breeds Corgis, too,' his wife added. 'They win at every show we go to.'

'Good for you.' Jennifer finally turned back to the registrar. 'You'll need to draw off blood for cultures, Doug. Then start fluid resus and antibiotics. What are you planning to use?'

'Gentamicin 5-7 milligrams per kilogram IV as a single daily dose, and amoxycillin 2 grams IV six-hourly.'

Jennifer nodded. 'Put a Foley catheter in. Get a urine sample and start monitoring output.' She turned back to her patient. 'I'll be back to see you later, Colin. Doug's going to look after you again now.'

The toddler was still screaming near the desk and an odd-looking man sat bolt upright on a stretcher beside the triage desk. A police office stood beside the ambulance crew.

'Hey…Jennifer!'

'Hi, Matt. What's brought you down here?' The orthopaedic consultant was not a frequent visitor to the emergency department.

'Overload. You've used up all my registrars. There's a nasty open femur and a fractured pelvis among the MVA patients that have come in. I'm just waiting for the X-rays to come through.'

'Oh.' Jennifer caught the eye of the triage nurse. 'Is the trauma room covered, Mel?'

'Yep. We've got a status 2 asthmatic coming in now, though. ETA two minutes. Can you cover that one?'

'Sure.' Jennifer's attention was again caught by the man on the stretcher, who was staring at Mel with an increasingly disgusted expression.

'Are you going to come out with us tonight?' Matt's voice was persuasive. 'You've been having early nights ever since you got back to work, and that's weeks ago now.'

'It's been tiring.' Jennifer turned her gaze to the over-full whiteboard listing the department's current patient load. No wonder beds were beginning to line up in the corridors. 'Maybe I should have taken more than a week to recover in the first place.'

'How's the arm?'

'No problem now. I just put a central line in and hardly noticed it.'

'And the feet?'

'Almost back to normal.' Jennifer was keeping one eye on the doors to the ambulance bay and another on a patient being moved from one of the resus areas. She would need that bed for the asthmatic patient coming in. 'I'm walking to work now but they're not up to dancing quite yet.'

'So just come to the drinks session and on to dinner. If you don't want to do the club thing after that, we'll let you go home.'

'I'll think about it,' Jennifer said evasively.

Matt's face fell. 'This isn't like you, Jen. The crowd's just not the same without you.'

Jennifer just smiled. Why was the invitation so un-appealing anyway? She had always worked hard and played hard, and a night on the town with a group of congenial people with exactly the same agenda had al-ways been the perfect way to wind down after a stressful shift. Right now, however, it came across as being an empty way to spend an evening. Shallow, even.

What would she rather be doing? Sitting in a hut in the middle of nowhere with a man who would have pre-ferred that she'd never set foot on his planet?

'Bitch!'

The vehement accusation was startling, but it wasn't directed at Jennifer. She whirled around to see the man on the stretcher still staring at Mel and making a vig-orous attempt to get up. Fortunately, the safety belt was restraining his hips and the police and ambulance offi-cers were quick enough to put pressure on his shoulders and force him back against the pillow.

'You're all the same,' the man shouted. 'You need to be wiped off the face of the bloody planet!'

Jennifer's eyes widened, but Matt grinned. 'I don't think he's too happy with the fairer sex at the moment, do you?'

Mel stepped hurriedly back behind the central counter. Jennifer stepped forward.

'What's going on?'

'Midazolam's wearing off,' the paramedic told her.

'History?'

'Police were called to a department store where he was slicing up women's clothing with a carving knife.' The paramedic raised an eyebrow. 'He was cross enough to be rather uncooperative. Seems that his girlfriend doesn't find his company too appealing anymore so she left…in the company of his best mate.'

The man on the stretcher spat on the floor near Jennifer's feet and struggled against the restraining hands. An IV pole crashed to the floor.

'Bitch!' he screamed again. 'It's *your* turn next!'

'Call Security,' Jennifer ordered. She caught the eye of a house surgeon emerging from a cubicle to see what the commotion was. 'Michelle, could you draw me up a 10 milligram dose of haloperidol, please? Matt, can you give us a hand? Mel, call Psych and tell them we need an urgent consult.'

The ambulance bay doors were sliding open and a young girl could be seen struggling for breath.

'Resus 3,' Jennifer called.

She pulled Doug from Resus 2 to help, leaving Matt and a very nervous house surgeon to deal with the psych patient.

'We need two secure IV lines,' she instructed Doug. 'Continuous nebulised salbutamol and aliquots of 0.1 milligrams adrenaline, IV. What's the oxygen saturation?'

'Less than ninety per cent,' the paramedic reported. 'We've got one patent IV. Sixteen gauge.'

'Good. Let's get her off the stretcher. Doug, get someone down from Anaesthetics. We may well need to intubate.'

'On the count of three,' someone said. 'One, two… three!'

'Sit her up,' Jennifer ordered. 'It's OK, sweetheart,' she told their patient. 'We'll get on top of this really soon.' She had her stethoscope in position, noting with dismay an almost silent chest and increasing panic in the girl. They were on the verge of a respiratory arrest. It was no problem to tune out the scream from behind the curtains.

'*Bitches!* You're all the same! Don't *touch* me! *Ah-h!*'

Twenty minutes later Jennifer's young asthmatic patient was on the way to the intensive care unit. Colin, the man with the septic shock from his urinary tract infection, had also gone to Intensive Care. The MVA victims were under control, two having gone to Theatre and one having a CT scan. The disturbed psychiatric patient was well sedated and had two burly security officers in attendance pending his transfer to a secure ward. Peter, the young man with the spontaneous pneumothorax, was still stable but the chance to grab a cup of coffee remained elusive.

'How long has the nosebleed been going on for?'

The epistaxis patient in Cubicle 7, Mrs Bennett, had presented enough of a challenge for a junior registrar to go in search of assistance. 'Over an hour,' she told Jennifer. 'And there's no response to direct pressure.'

'Spontaneous bleed?'

'Started after she sneezed.'

'Any past history?'

'Not of nosebleeds. She has hypertension and angina. She's on aspirin, 300 milligrams a day.'

'That won't be helping. Is the bleeding anterior or posterior?'

The registrar looked disconcerted. 'I'm not sure. Presumably posterior, if direct pressure isn't enough to control it.'

'Get a Y suction catheter,' Jennifer instructed. 'And find out where the site of bleeding is. When the catheter is passed beyond the bleeding site you'll get blood appearing at the nostrils again.'

The registrar nodded.

'Take bloods for haemoglobin, blood group and a co-agulation profile. What's the blood pressure?'

'One-ten over 60.'

'And she's normally hypertensive?''

'Yes. She's on a beta-blocker for that.'

'Keep a close eye on her, then. With beta blockade, she won't be showing a rise in heart rate to warn you of hypovolaemia. Get IV access and put fluids up.'

'Will it need packing?'

'Get back to me when you've decided on the bleeding point. If it's posterior and still severe, we might need to use a Foley's catheter in combination with anterior pack-ing. She'll probably need some sedation to cope with that. She'll also need antibiotics if it's packed, and we'll have to admit her.'

A nurse hurried up, holding a cardboard container. 'Mrs Bennett's just vomited.' She held out the bowl which appeared to contain a large volume of fresh blood.

Jennifer started moving rapidly towards Cubicle 7. 'Mel? Could you get someone from ENT to come down, please?'

Staff from the ear, nose and throat department were not readily available, which would have been a nuisance for Jennifer a few weeks ago, keeping her tied to the treatment of a single patient and unavailable for the next critical case to come through the doors. The satisfaction to be gained from focussing on one patient was a new phenomenon, but the change in the way Professor Allen worked had not gone unnoticed.

'Are you going visiting this afternoon?' Mel held up a pair of spectacles. 'Only these are Mr Smith's glasses and if you're going up to ICU, I won't have to find an orderly to deliver them.'

Jennifer took the spectacles. 'I'll pop up and see how he's getting on after my shift finishes.' She glanced at the wall clock. 'Which should be in about ten minutes.'

It was actually more like an hour. What should have been a swift final consult to finish her day, as she saw the toddler who'd been screaming intermittently for half the afternoon and prescribed antibiotics for an angry ear infection, was hijacked by the distraught mother of a fourteen-year-old girl.

There were no staff members immediately available to talk to the quietly sobbing woman so Jennifer took her into the relatives' room herself and closed the door.

'You're Courtney's mother, aren't you?'

She nodded. 'I'm Jane. They've just taken Courtney to the operating theatre.'

'She needs a D and C,' Jennifer explained gently. 'The miscarriage wasn't complete.'

'I didn't even know she was pregnant. I had no idea! I should have known.' Tears flowed afresh. 'And she'd been raped at a party. Why didn't she *tell* me?'

'Sometimes, when something terrible happens, it's easier to try and pretend it didn't happen than to have to go over and over it in your head. Telling someone forces you to confront the reality, and that's a hard thing to do.'

Jennifer hadn't spoken to her colleagues or even close friends in any detail about her experience of the plane crash. Maybe that was why it was proving so difficult to stop thinking about it all. About the narrow brush with death. About losing a patient she had desperately wanted to save. About the ordeal of the long trek to safety.

About Guy Knight.

'I should have known something had happened. I just thought she'd fallen out with her friends at school or she was worried about exams or something. She's been so quiet for the last few weeks. Not eating or sleeping properly. Not going out with her mates.'

It sounded remarkably familiar to Jennifer. She hadn't been raped, of course—quite the opposite—but the terror of the crash and its aftermath had to rank fairly highly in any list of traumatic events.

'You'll get through this,' Jennifer said reassuringly. 'It'll take time and it might not be easy, but your daughter needs your support now more than ever.'

Jane sniffed and then nodded. 'I would have been there for her, even if she'd ended up having the baby. Except…how could you love the child if the father had done *that?* This is probably the best thing that could have happened. That's an awful thing to say, isn't it?'

'It's a perfectly understandable reaction,' Jennifer assured her. 'And now Courtney's got the chance to put it behind her and move on with her life. With your support.'

It was just as well Jennifer hadn't ended up with any kind of reminder more tangible than memories. It hadn't even occurred to her at the time that she was risking pregnancy…or worse. Jennifer *never* took risks like that. She must have been out of her mind. She had been lucky but it had been stupid, and Jennifer didn't try to push back the anger her stupidity generated even now.

'I'd like to be there when she wakes up.'

'They'll let you into the recovery room. It shouldn't take long. A D and C is a fairly quick procedure.'

'Can I go there now?'

'I don't see why not.' Jennifer stood up. 'I'm on my way to the intensive care unit so I go past Recovery. I'll show you the way and have a word with the nursing staff.' Anger was dulling into a vague irritation and movement seemed like a good way to dispel the negative mood.

Their progress along the corridor was temporarily blocked by a patient being moved with a large entourage of medical attendants. They were manoeuvring the bed with extreme care and Jennifer could see that they had an unstable spinal injury patient, probably on the way to Theatre or Intensive Care. The young male had his head secured in halo traction and was on a ventilator.

'Motorbikes,' the accompanying consultant muttered as he passed Jennifer. 'Don't you love them? C4-5 fracture.' He turned his head again a moment later. 'Only two weeks to go, Jennifer. Still confident?'

'As always, John.' Jennifer's smile felt forced. John's looked smug.

'May the best *man* win and all that.'

The journey with Courtney's mother continued in silence. John was the main competition Jennifer faced in the upcoming decision regarding a new head of department for Auckland Central's emergency department. A few years older than Jennifer, he was amused by her bid for the top job and rarely missed any opportunity to put her in what he considered to be her place.

Common dislike of John's arrogance might well work in her favour, she decided a little later, having finally left the hospital after confirming that Colin was responding to treatment and his condition improving. Her chin rose unconsciously as she started the short walk to her apartment. The nagging irritation that the talk with Courtney's mother had generated now had new fuel. She'd show her fellow consultant. She'd win this position, and when she did, she'd do something about the way John interacted with both his colleagues and his patients.

*   *   *

It was a Friday evening, and the cafés and bars in the trendy commercial area of Jennifer's apartment were all buzzing. She walked past people sitting at tables on the pavement, and a wave of nausea swept over her at the rich aroma of roasted meat. Ducking down her alley, she punched in the security code for the gate and ran upstairs to let herself into her apartment and get to the bathroom just in time.

With a facecloth soaked in cold water and pressed to the back of her neck, Jennifer stared at her pale reflection in the mirror. What on earth was wrong with her? She was probably hypoglycaemic, she decided. It had been a physically stressful day and she hadn't eaten anything other than the biscuit with a cup of tea at some point late in the morning. She often got through a hard day without a meal, but she hadn't had her usual breakfast this morning, had she? The thought of food had made her feel queasy even then.

Jennifer hoped she wasn't coming down with some kind of virus. She needed to be on top form in the run-up to this job interview, and she was already at a disadvantage with her broken arm and the general tiredness she couldn't quite shake off. It was just as well she had declined the invitation for a night out on the town. What she needed was a hot bath, some good food and an early night before another 6:00 a.m. start tomorrow.

Soaking in scented water, Jennifer started mentally ticking off the day's cases. Often only a couple stood out and the rest became an easily forgotten blur unless her memory was jogged. For some reason, not being able to remember the details of all of them, or put a name or face to a case, had become disheartening over the last couple of weeks.

Peter was easy to remember because he'd reminded her of Guy. Colin had made her think of Digger. The psych patient with his desire for revenge against all women was certainly memorable and that toddler with the ear infection had been called something a little unusual. India? No, Africa. The name of an elderly woman with a fractured neck of femur had vanished completely, however, and Jennifer sighed, giving up the game. Maybe she was just pushing herself too hard at the moment in her determination to slot back into the routine of her normal life and create the kind of impression that would help her win the coveted position of head of department.

Keeping her cast dry while bathing had become part of the daily routine, but Jennifer was looking forward to having it removed. She was due for another X-ray on Monday, which would be four weeks since the fracture. At least it wasn't painful any longer. Just irritating.

Like not being able to remember the name of that old woman. The one who'd slipped while mopping her kitchen floor. Gloria? Gladys? When the hairbrush slipped from her hand a moment later, Jennifer actually swore aloud. Then she shook her head and laughed at herself. Being irritable and snappy denoted a lack of control that had never been a fault of hers, and she wasn't going to tolerate it now. What she needed was a glass of wine to wash away the nagging sense of unease that seemed to be plaguing her.

John wasn't worth wasting emotional energy on. Except that this mood had started before that meeting in the corridor, hadn't it? She'd been angered by the reminder of what she'd risked by that night with Guy. Nearly a month ago.

Let it go, she told herself. It's over.

Except that it wasn't, was it?

Jennifer stared at her glass of wine but she didn't raise it to her lips. The irritation left in the wake of the conversation with Courtney's mother had had nothing to do with her own stupidity regarding that night. She had been stupid all right, but it was the continuance of that state providing the irritation now. She had been a perfect example of the kind of denial she had described to Courtney's mother, but the awareness of what had been provoked was only just surfacing now.

She'd taken a risk and maybe she *hadn't* been so lucky. It was four weeks ago now. The stress of the whole experience might not be enough to explain why her period was a little late. And two weeks couldn't be considered a *little* late anymore either.

'Oh, my God,' Jennifer breathed.

Was it possible she was *pregnant?* With *Guy Knight*'s baby?

It was easy enough to find out. A quick trip to the staff toilet with a testing kit at 6:00 a.m. the next day confirmed the suspicion that had kept Jennifer awake for most of the night.

The shock would have been numbing except that it didn't have much of a chance to set in. Jennifer was still washing her hands when a nurse burst into the rest room.

'Oh, *there* you are, Dr Allen. We've got an arrest in Resus 2 and there's a multi-victim MVA arriving any minute.'

'On my way.' The crumpled paper towels fell into the rubbish bin and covered an equally crumpled pregnancy test kit.

Jennifer almost stopped in her tracks on entering Resus

2. Why, of all days, did she have to face a case like this right now?

'Apparently found non-breathing fifteen minutes ago,' Doug informed her. 'CPR started by the ambulance crew.'

Even the tiny paediatric defibrillator paddles looked far too large to be used and the tube securing the airway of this patient obscenely out of place.

'How old is she?'

'Ten weeks.'

It was sadly clearly too late for this baby but they had to go through the motions.

'Shocking again. Everybody clear?'

'Clear.'

'Where are the parents?' Jennifer had taken over the bag-mask ventilation. It took only a gentle squeeze to inflate tiny lungs. The main reason for going through a distressing process like this was to reassure distraught parents that everything possible was being done for their child, but there were no stricken bystanders in Resus 2.

'The mother's in a cubicle.' Doug sounded disgusted as he drew up new drugs. 'Too drunk to stand up. The father's being interviewed by the police.' He watched the compressions on the tiny chest in front of him. 'She's seventeen. He's just out of prison. There was a party going on and apparently the baby was making too much noise. Mother says she put her in their bed and didn't notice she wasn't breathing until she woke up this morning.'

Had the infant been inadvertently suffocated, sleeping with an intoxicated adult, or had something more sinister happened earlier in the night? It would be up to the pathologist and police to determine the cause of death, but maybe it was actually an escape from a bleak future for this child. Jennifer glanced at the clock.

'How long has CPR been in progress?'

'Forty-five minutes, including pre-hospital time.'

'I'm calling it, then, if we're all in agreement,' Jennifer said heavily. 'Doug?'

'Yeah.' The registrar shook his head, his face grim.

'Michelle?'

The house surgeon just nodded.

'Suzy?'

The nurse also nodded mutely, her eyes filling with tears.

'OK. Time of death 6:45 a.m.' Jennifer's gaze returned to the infant, a tiny still shape on the bed. She reached to disconnect the ECG electrodes. It would be nice to remove the ET tube, but the pathologist would need to confirm its correct placement and maybe there wouldn't be a parent wanting to hold this baby immediately anyway.

'Dr Allen?' A head came through the gap in the curtains. 'They need you in the trauma room.'

'Be there in a second.' Jennifer stripped off her gloves. It was better that she had to focus on something else right now. Otherwise the overwhelming sadness would be too much and she might totally ruin her chances of becoming the head of this department by being seen weeping in a corner somewhere.

She flicked the curtain back to screen the area as she emerged into an already humming department. Straightening her spine, Jennifer set off to deal with the rest of her shift. She could cope. She had to.

She was in control of the destiny of more than one person now. Her baby was never going to lie abandoned on some hospital bed. It would be loved and cared for to the very best of her ability. Maybe it *was* a shock to be facing motherhood like this, but there was no doubt whatsoever in Jennifer's mind that she couldn't find a way around any of the problems it might create.

Yes. She *wanted* this baby.

As the days passed over the next week, tentative ideas became plans. She would have to leave her apartment, of course. A child needed a real home, with a garden, preferably close to a good school. She wouldn't be able to manage alone, but that wasn't an insurmountable problem either. She would be able to afford the best available in nannies, especially if she became the head of department.

The upcoming interview had provided several days of anxious focus and had interfered more than a little with her concentration levels but it, too, settled into the shape of a plan. As long as nobody found out about her condition before the interview, it shouldn't make any difference. She could always plead ignorance later and blame it on something like an irregular cycle or a lighter than normal period. Sure, she might need some time off but if it all went well, she could work right up until she was due, and if she saved up all her paid leave she could probably take a month off before coming back to work full time.

But what about Guy?

The issue had been there from the moment she'd seen the colour appear on the test strip, but it kept getting pushed to the bottom of the list as she sorted through all the other worries. There was no avoiding it now, although Jennifer managed to put it aside for just a little longer while she made a quick trip to a medical ward to finish her day.

Colin Smith reminded her even more of Digger today, with his tufty hair in disarray but a cheeky smile on his face.

'It's my angel back again.'

'You're looking so much better.' Jennifer's delight was obvious. 'Are they letting you go home soon?'

'Tomorrow.'

'That's wonderful.'

Jennifer headed for home feeling very satisfied. She had to weave her way through a very busy street, with people enjoying a sunny Saturday evening at the cafés and boutique shops. Traffic was snarled up at one point, with drivers hooting in irritation. A teenage girl, texting on her cell phone without looking up, bumped Jennifer's shoulder as she passed. Collecting her balance, she spotted a dark head at one of the footpath tables. For a split second, Jennifer was convinced it was Guy.

Turning into the alleyway leading to her apartment block, Jennifer saw the man's profile and realised it wasn't Guy. A curious mixture of relief and disappointment stayed with her as she climbed the stairs and an image of the real man was uppermost in her mind.

Opening a window to air the apartment, all the sounds and smells of the street below came inside and Jennifer suddenly felt more than disappointed. She felt…trapped.

Lost.

She would rather be sitting beside a picture-perfect mountain lake, she realised with something like desperation. Absorbing the stillness. Waiting for Guy to return.

Sitting down, she tried to pull herself together but nothing worked. The plans she had been formulating all week were no longer the answer to any problems. They all felt suddenly wrong. The satisfaction in following up one of her patients today to find him due for discharge evaporated. Could she even remember half the cases she had seen today? Would she have the time or inclination to follow any of *them* up?

She was tired. Bone-achingly weary. Closing her eyes and dropping her head onto the back of the couch, Jennifer allowed herself to focus on the only thing that really mattered right now.

She was going to have a baby.

Would it be a girl with blonde hair and blue eyes like her? Maybe it would be a boy with dark eyes and a flop of even darker hair. Like his father.

And with that thought, Jennifer sighed. There was no way around this. A telephone call or a letter to inform Guy of his impending fatherhood wasn't good enough. He wouldn't welcome Jennifer coming into his life again but she had the perfect excuse now, didn't she? Telling someone news like this could only decently be done face to face.

A knot of excitement coalesced amidst the emotional turmoil. All the half-formed fantasies and even the crazy idea she could be in love with the man of the mountains that Jennifer had attributed to post-traumatic stress syndrome edged back into her mind. If she saw him again, she would know exactly how she really felt, wouldn't she?

She wouldn't tell him she was coming. She wouldn't even need to tell anyone at the hospital where she was going. The mission could be accomplished on her next couple of days off. And maybe, just maybe Guy might be happy to see her again. He might even welcome the idea of becoming a father if it was forced on him.

Never mind those emphatic statements he had made about not planning on having kids and having no space in his life for them. It was another remembered comment that seemed of far greater significance at this moment. What had that woman said in the eavesdropped conversation? 'If anyone needs a family, that young man does.'

Jennifer was unaware of the tears trickling down her face. *She* needed a family, too. A complete family. Something she hadn't had since she was eight years old. Was that what the appeal of having a baby was all about? That she would have someone to love who would love her back?

But it wasn't just the baby she wanted, was it?

Jennifer wanted Guy as well.

CHAPTER EIGHT

ESCAPE was no longer an option.

By the time Guy had seen who was sitting on his doorstep there was no way he could follow his instincts, turn around and drive away like the proverbial bat out of hell.

Jennifer Allen was the last person he had expected— or *wanted*—to see again. Especially now, just when he was finally starting to piece his life back together again.

Tearing an incredulous stare away from the figure of his unwanted visitor, Guy drove straight past the entrance to his home, through the archway in the old macrocarpa hedge and into the corrugated-iron shed that served as a garage. With the engine on his four-wheel-drive Toyota silent, the sound of the rain beating on the tin roof was obvious, but it didn't even occur to Guy to hurry and rescue the person sheltering from the weather under the overhang of his small porch.

Nearly seven weeks had passed since that fateful sightseeing flight. Six weeks since Guy had attended the funeral marking the end of the most significant chapter of his life. He had witnessed the burial of the closest person he'd had to a remaining family member and, as far as he was concerned, any fallout from the crash and his brief encounter with Professor Jennifer Allen had been buried right along with Digger.

Now she was *here* and even a glimpse had brought everything rushing back. Guy didn't realise he had his eyes screwed tightly shut or that his hands were bunched

into fists. It was the anxious whine from the back seat
of the car that snapped him into focussing on the present
again.

'It's OK, guys.' The soothing tone was automatic. 'I'll
sort it.'

Climbing down from the driver's seat, Guy opened
the back door and his two dogs jumped clear of the
vehicle. Jake, the sleek black retriever, shoved his nose
into Guy's hand and Jessie, his golden counterpart, cir-
cled his legs. Both animals could clearly sense his tension and Guy grinned as he scratched a set of golden
ears and then black ones.

'I'm not really bothered,' he lied. 'We're through the
worst of all this, so it isn't going to make that much
difference, is it?'

The dogs grinned back, tongues lolling and dark eyes
offering all the comfort he might need. They were in
complete agreement but Guy knew they were all kidding
themselves. Of course seeing Jennifer would make a difference. The unknown factor was just how much of the
healing would be scraped painfully away.

Guy turned up the collar of his oilskin coat and
hunched his shoulders as he headed towards the curtain
of rain screening the open side of the shed. It had been
such a struggle to get as far as he had in the last few
weeks. Grief had stalked him constantly, ready to take
over at unexpected moments and sabotage whatever
progress he'd thought he was making. Nightmares of the
actual crash and the horror of watching Digger die had
made sleep an undesirable necessity for weeks.

Fantasies involving the feel and even taste of
Jennifer's body had added an even more unwelcome di-
mension to a state of emotional upheaval. Juxtaposed
with grief, memories of this woman had taken on a dis-

honourable—even shameful—aura. That was why he had never wanted to see her again, and that was what was uppermost in his mind as he approached his house.

'Hullo, Jenna,' he said stiffly. 'What the hell are you doing here?'

She looked cold. A soft-looking black woollen coat was pulled around her shoulders and covered her as far as the top of what had to be a replacement pair of long black boots, but her face was pinched and rather pale. Her smile looked forced as well, but that could be due to his unwelcoming tone as much as the cold.

'Hello, Guy.' Jennifer stood up. 'Sorry. I do realise this is a bit of a surprise for you. I…ah…wanted to talk to you.'

The dogs moved from sentry duty on either side of Guy to investigate the stranger. Jake offered a paw that left a muddy streak on the elegant black coat, but Guy wasn't about to apologise or reprimand his pet.

'I do have a telephone.'

'I didn't have your number.'

'You seem to have found my address.'

'That wasn't hard.' Jennifer was looking down at the dogs who were both now sitting in front of her, plumed tails waving a greeting. A genuine smile tweaked the corners of her mouth 'I dropped in at the Glenfalloch pub and told the woman behind the bar that I was a friend of yours but I'd lost the directions for finding your house.' The sentence was broken by a bout of shivering. 'Would it be possible to go inside, do you think? I'm freezing.'

Guy said nothing as he stepped past her to open the door.

'I thought it would be locked,' Jennifer exclaimed. 'I didn't think of trying it.'

'No.' Guy's tone was dry. 'I don't suppose you leave doors unlocked where you come from.'

Jennifer ignored the attempt to make her feel displaced. 'The woman at the pub was very helpful and there was a man with an astonishingly big white beard that drew me a map on the back of a coaster.'

Guy had picked up an old towel lying beside the collection of outdoor footwear on the flagstones and was busy drying dog paws. He would be having a word with both Maureen and Mack in the near future. They had probably recognised Jennifer thanks to her having had her face splashed all over the newspapers, and half the community probably knew by now that she was visiting. Maybe they were all wondering, as he was, why on earth she had come back.

'Bit of a stretch of the imagination, calling us friends, wasn't it?'

'Seemed as good a word as any.'

Guy rose from his crouch and met her stare. It certainly wasn't coming from a stranger, the way it touched something deep inside that he had no wish to identify. A space he'd never known existed, in fact. There was no denying they had a bond. Maybe any fellow survivors of a disaster had that. Or maybe it had sprung from a night of pretending they were lovers. Whatever it was, it was unsettling.

Dangerous.

'You'd better come in, then.' Guy opened a heavy wooden door and the warmth from the coal range in the cottage kitchen drew an exclamation of pleasure from Jennifer. She walked straight towards the source of the warmth but her head was turning from side to side as she gazed at her surroundings.

'This is gorgeous,' she pronounced. 'It's really old, isn't it?'

'This part is the original settler's cottage. The stone walls are over half a metre thick. There have been additions, of course, but they've all been made in keeping with the style and trying to use the same materials.' Guy bypassed the kitchen to head for the large open fireplace where he set a match to the crumpled newspaper and pine cones in the grate.

He waited until the kindling caught and then added some larger pieces of firewood. He was taken back instantly to the night beside that lake, where he'd made the fire that had probably kept them both from succumbing to hypothermia. The memory of caring for her feet only served as a reminder of how much more intimately he had touched this woman. Guy bent a thick branch across his knee until it snapped, making a crack that resounded off the thick walls of the cottage like gunfire.

Jessie cringed and wagged her tail apologetically and Guy ruffled her head in reassurance. The touch grounded him enough to shake off those dangerous memories and he straightened, brushing dust from his hands.

'How's your arm?' he enquired politely. 'I see you've got rid of the cast already.' Jennifer had taken her coat off and draped it over one of the spindle-backed chairs surrounding the old kauri table.

'It was a clean break and it healed fast.' Jennifer was looking at her hand as she flexed her fingers. 'I'll just need to make sure I don't stress it too much for a few more weeks.' She looked up. 'How's the ankle?'

'Fine. It was only a hairline fracture. I think Hugh insisted on putting it in a cast just to slow me down a bit. Anyway, I took it tramping again last week and it held up.' Guy ducked automatically as he walked under the huge beam that separated the low ceiling of the living area from the lean-to kitchen. He filled an old cast-iron kettle with water and put it on top of the coal range, then turned his attention to finding coffee mugs.

Last week's excursion had marked the real turning point in Guy's recovery. The trip to what had been a favourite haunt for both himself and Digger, deep in the wilds of Fiordland, had been gruelling, both physically and emotionally, but it had also been exactly what he'd needed.

With no one to hear sobs torn from his soul, he had been able to give his grief free rein and come to terms with the fact that he was, for the first time in his life, completely alone in the world. And there had been a kind of peace to be found in the knowledge. He was responsible for only his own happiness and he would find that again in his work and community. In his home, his pets and especially in his surroundings.

He belonged here. Any errant thoughts of attempting city life again in order to re-establish contact with Jennifer could be dismissed as the kind of reckless dependence on another person that had created such deep misery in the past. And the present, given the depth of his grief at losing Digger.

Guy spooned coffee into the mugs. 'Do you take milk?'

'No, thanks. Just black. No sugar either.'

He set the mugs on the table and sat down. The sooner they got this over with, the sooner he could reclaim the kind of peace he'd found on that solitary walk. But Jennifer didn't seem to be in any hurry to get to the point of this visit and the silence began to feel uncomfortable.

'So…' Guy cleared his throat. 'You're back at work, then?'

'Of course. I only took a week off.'

'Busy?'

'Very. What about you?'

'Average workload. It wouldn't impress you but it keeps me busy enough.' Guy swallowed a mouthful of his coffee. 'I've been helping out for a day or two every week in Bill's practice in Te Anau. It took a while to find a locum.'

'It must have been a shock for the community.'

'Yeah. The town virtually closed for the funeral.'

'And Digger's? Was there a good turnout for him?'

'Yeah.' Guy could feel a poignant pride shaping his smile. The whole area had contributed to Digger's send-off. The aero club had done a fly-past in formation. The Glenfalloch pub had put on an amazing spread and so many people had had stories to tell that the wake had gone on well into the night.

'I wish I'd stayed.'

'You would have felt out of place.' Guy pushed his mug away and let his gaze rest heavily on Jennifer. This was getting them nowhere fast. 'Why are you here?' he said finally. 'Do you want to visit the crash site or something so you can put it all behind you and get on with real life?'

'I'm never going to be able to put it all behind me. It's changed my life.'

'Oh?' Guy couldn't help sounding sceptical. 'A brush with death and you've seen the light, then?'

'In a way.' Jennifer was toying with her mug, her fingers stroking the rim in slow circles. Guy had to look away. 'I'm going to be making a few changes.' She looked up and Guy could see resolution in her eyes.

'That's why I'm here,' she said quietly. 'I wanted to discuss them with you.'

'What for?' Surprise sharpened his tone. 'I'm not part of your life, Jenna. I never expected to even see you again. Your plans have nothing to do with me.' Something like alarm was kicking him in the belly, creating a knot that was nothing like the one watching Jennifer's fingers stroking that mug had provoked.

'Actually, my plans might have quite a lot to do with you, Guy.' Jennifer held his gaze and he could read a mix of emotions along with that resolution now. Fear perhaps? Sympathy even?

'You…' Jennifer had to clear her throat before she spoke again. 'You're the father of the baby I'm carrying, Guy.'

Please, God, *no!*

This couldn't be happening. It wasn't real. The ringing of the telephone, now, *that* was real. Guy pushed back his chair and stood up, pleased to find his legs still working despite the curious numbing effect Jennifer's statement had induced. His voice was still working, too, which seemed surprising, given the tightness in his throat.

'Guy Knight.' He listened for few seconds. 'Calm down, Ellie. What's happened?' He listened again. 'How far apart are the pains? Have you called the ambulance? OK. I'm on my way.'

It was a relief to push aside what had to be confronted. 'I've got to go,' he told Jennifer tersely. 'It's an emergency.' He walked swiftly towards the fire to put the guard in place. 'We'll talk later.'

'I'll come with you.'

'No.'

'Why not?' Jennifer was following him. The dogs were following her. 'It's an emergency. I'm an emergency physician. I might be able to help.'

'No. I can manage, thanks.'

'What kind of emergency is it?' Jennifer was totally ignoring him, pulling on her long, black coat.

Guy flicked her a dark glance. 'Premature delivery,' he snapped.

'Oh.' The significance clearly wasn't lost on Jennifer. She bit her lip as she offered him a tiny smile. 'Bit close to home, huh?'

It was that tentative smile that changed things. She understood his shock. Given the kind of control Jennifer liked to exert on her life, she'd probably been just as shocked—if not more so—when she'd discovered she was pregnant. Her life, possibly her whole career, was in for a major shake-up. Maybe she had been as reluctant as he was to renew their acquaintance, but decency had brought her here to tell him the news face to face.

And somewhere deep inside a seed of something like joy was planted with the knowledge that he was going to become a father. He would have a connection to another human being that meant he wasn't as totally alone in the world as he had thought.

'Come on, then,' he growled. 'We're wasting time.'

Jennifer had her seat belt fastened by the time the dogs scrambled into the back seat.

'What's the history?' she queried.

'Ellie's thirty-eight and this is her first pregnancy. She's thirty-five weeks into it. We've been keeping a close eye on her because she had a mild to moderate degree of placenta previa.'

'Was the conception normal?'

Guy snorted. 'I haven't gone into the details. She and

Phil have been married for fifteen years so I imagine they've had a bit of practice.'

Jennifer wasn't smiling. 'Being close to forty is quite old for a first baby. I just wondered if they'd had fertility treatment like IVF.'

Guy turned off the shingled lane that led to his cottage and picked up speed on the sealed road. 'Fair enough. Yes, they've been trying for a baby ever since they married. IVF isn't really an option for people in isolated areas who are struggling to earn a living anyway.'

'And what's happening at the moment?'

'She's in severe pain and is bleeding.' Guy pushed his foot down more firmly on the accelerator. 'The ambulance and the helicopter are both involved with a car-versus-train incident at Kingston. It'll be at least forty minutes before they can get here.'

'Where are we going?'

'Not too far, fortunately. We cross the Matukituki river into West Wanaka and then head up the valley. We've got a ford and a few farm gates to get through.'

Jennifer needed no prompting to leap out and open the first gate. When she didn't need to be reminded to close it again, Guy remembered that she was a townie by choice rather than upbringing. He still didn't expect her reaction when the second gate was blocked by the farm's largest bull.

The huge animal refused to budge when Jennifer tried to push the gate open. Having been chased by a similar brute when he was ten years old, Guy would never have done what Jennifer did now. With her coat flapping and her skirt hitched up to her thighs, she simply climbed over one end of the gate. Picking up a long branch from beneath the pine trees that flanked the driveway, she marched towards the bull and gave him an almighty whack on the rump.

'Move it,' she ordered. 'We need to get through.'

The bull was as surprised as Guy had been. It skittered clumsily to one side but then seemed to regroup and glared balefully at Jennifer as she opened the gate. Guy drove through as the gap widened but the bull was moving again and looked as though he might get through before the gate cut off the road to freedom.

Jennifer was having none of it. She raced behind the Toyota, seemingly oblivious to the muddy puddles soaking her boots and splattering her coat. The branch looked like a lethal weapon as she wielded it and her angry shouts would certainly have been enough to prevent Guy trying to annoy her further. He was grinning as she climbed back into the vehicle.

'I wouldn't want to be one of your registrars standing in the wrong place.'

Jennifer pushed sopping wet tendrils of hair behind her ears. She grinned back. 'Haven't had to hit anyone with a stick for a while, but I'll keep it in mind. It was quite fun.'

There was nothing fun about the scene that greeted them at the farmhouse. Ellie lay on the floor beside her telephone, doubled over in pain, with a bloodstain soaking her clothing and an ominous puddle creeping out over the linoleum.

'Have you got shears in here?' Jennifer was already unclipping the catches on Guy's large medical kit. 'We'd better get those clothes off.'

'Who's she?' Ellie was clinging to Guy's hand.

'Her name's Jennifer,' Guy told her. 'She's an emergency specialist from Auckland.' He squeezed her hand.

'Thought I might need some backup so I ordered her in.'

'I'm scared, Guy,' Ellie sobbed. 'I'm going to lose the baby, aren't I?'

'Not if we can help it.' Jennifer handed the shears to Guy then paused to smile at Ellie. 'How long ago did the bleeding start?'

'Just before I rang Guy. The pains started at the same time and—ah-h!' Another contraction made the effort to speak too great.

'I'll start an IV, shall I?' Jennifer queried. 'Ellie could do with some pain relief.' Her glance towards the spreading puddle of blood on the floor was pointed. 'And some fluids.'

Guy nodded, busy cutting away a pair of maternity jeans and underwear. His gloves were heavily blood-stained before he even touched his patient. 'We've got a foot and leg through the cervix,' he said seconds later.

'What does that mean?' Ellie cried in panic.

'Your baby's almost here,' Guy responded. 'And he's decided to come out backwards. I'm going to find his other foot and give him a hand.'

'But it's too early,' Ellie wailed.

'Are you allergic to any drugs that you know of?' Jennifer asked.

'No...I don't know... Guy, what are you *doing?* Ah-h!'

The need for pain relief abated as Guy eased the baby's forearm clear of its shoulder. He grasped the baby's ankles and swung upwards, and the second arm appeared.

'Take a deep breath, Ellie,' he said calmly. 'You're doing well. We're almost there.'

The warning glance from Jennifer was unnecessary

but Guy nodded anyway. The head of a breech delivery had to be as slow as possible to decrease risk of damage to skull membranes by sudden decompression and release.

'Sharp scratch, Ellie.' Jennifer had a bag of IV fluids and a giving set beside her, ready to hook up as soon as the cannula was in place. 'Blood pressure's 100 on 55,' she murmured to Guy. With another glance at the blood around them, she added softly, 'Not bad at all really.'

Guy was concentrating on his own task. He eased the baby back over Ellie's abdomen, the tiny arms dangling as he helped the head negotiate its narrow exit. A rush of new blood loss accompanied the completion of the delivery, but Guy's attention was still caught by the flaccid baby.

'I'll take him.' Somehow Jennifer had located the suction bulb, the paediatric bag mask and a clean towel. She handed him the clips for the umbilical cord and then took the infant and placed it on the towel. She suctioned the airway and then gently inflated the baby's lungs with the bag mask.

Ellie was struggling to sit up. 'Oh, my God,' she cried. 'He's dead, isn't he?'

'No.' Jennifer's tone was firm. 'He's got a pulse. It's just not very strong yet and he's not quite ready to breathe so I'm helping him.'

'We've still got some bleeding going on here.' Guy reached for his kit. 'I'm going to see if we can help the placenta along with some oxytocin.'

'Why am I bleeding?' Ellie's gaze was fixed on her baby in horror as Jennifer worked over it.

'Your placenta wasn't in a great position, as we knew. When your cervix started to dilate, part of it tore away from the lining of your uterus. You may have been in labour for a while without noticing.'

'I had a sore back all night. I thought it was the way I was lying.' Ellie was now looking at the blood on the floor. 'I hope I'm not bleeding to death here,' she said fearfully.

'It looks a lot worse than it is,' Guy said reassuringly. 'It's amazing how far a bit of blood can spread, especially on lino. I'd estimate you've lot about a bit more than a litre but we've got some extra fluid going in to replace it and the bleeding should stop as soon as the placenta is delivered and the vessels constrict. This drug I'm giving you will speed things up.'

'I feel sick,' Ellie moaned.

'Have you got a pressure cuff you can put on the fluids?' Jennifer asked.

'Yes. I'll get another line in, too.'

'Good.' Jennifer's tone indicated satisfaction with more than Guy's plan. 'That's the way, wee man,' she said. 'Look…he's taken his first breath by himself! He's pinking up already.'

Sure enough, the baby was showing signs of life finally. Guy just hoped it was soon enough for no permanent damage to have been caused by oxygen depletion. Given Jennifer's intense efforts, it was highly unlikely and Guy was acutely aware that he couldn't have looked after both mother and child alone. If Ellie's longed-for baby survived this difficult birth unscathed, it would be entirely to Jennifer's credit.

Ellie seemed to realise that as well. Wrapped in a towel, with his eyes open, the tiny boy was in his mother's arms only minutes later as Jennifer helped Ellie hold her son.

'He's gorgeous,' Jennifer told her. 'And he seems

fine. He's a good weight for thirty-five weeks, too. I don't think he'll even need to go into an incubator.'

'Thank you,' Ellie sobbed. 'Thank you so much. I don't care what happens to me—it was the baby I was scared about.'

Jennifer and Guy cared about what happened to Ellie. With the delivery of the placenta, her haemorrhage finally slowed and stopped, but she was shocked enough to need constant monitoring, and Jennifer was clearly as pleased as Guy to see the arrival of the ambulance crew.

'Ellie, this isn't fair!' The flame-haired paramedic, Maggie, was shaking her head. 'We had an agreement. We were going to go hooning over the Crown Range with lights and sirens on at the first sign of labour.' She bent over the bundle in Ellie's arms. 'Oh...' she breathed. 'I *want* one.'

'You'll have to get your own.' Ellie smiled. 'This one's mine.'

'And mine.' The man who burst into the room now was white-faced and totally soaked. 'Ellie, are you all right?'

'She will be,' Guy told Phil. 'We need to get to hospital now, though. She's lost a fair bit of blood.'

'And the baby? Is it OK?'

'Thanks to Dr Allen, he is,' Ellie told him. 'I thought he was dead.' Tears of happiness were rolling down her cheeks. 'She saved him for us, Phil.'

Jennifer was subjected to an appraising and then very appreciative stare.

'I don't know how to thank you in that case, Dr Allen,' Phil said.

Jennifer smiled. 'Call me Jenna. And I was more than happy to be able to help.'

Phil, Maggie and her crew partner exchanged glances

and Guy found himself smiling along with them. If Jennifer had wanted to orchestrate a way of finding instant acceptance into this community, she couldn't have come up with a better way than being instrumental in the successful delivery of a new—and long awaited—member. Absurdly, he felt proud of her. Proud of her skills with resuscitating the baby and proud that she had already won a place in the hearts of the people he lived and worked with. It was a dangerous line of thought. He didn't want Jennifer to feel welcome here, because she *wasn't*. Not as far as he was concerned.

Phil was now staring at his son. He reached out but it was to touch his wife's head, not the baby's. 'Are you really OK, hon?'

The look that passed between the couple made everyone else in the room superfluous. Guy had the curious sensation of witnessing the birth of a family as Ellie and Phil bowed their heads over the baby. He swallowed hard as he glanced at Jennifer. If he could feel like this at the birth of someone else's child, how would he feel when it came time for the birth of his own?

Vulnerable. That's how he would feel. Responsible for the happiness of someone other than himself. Someone whose upbringing would be under the control of someone other than himself. It was a recipe for emotional disaster, that's what it was.

Guy had to escape before he got sucked in any deeper.

CHAPTER NINE

'Do you go in for dramatic entrances, then?'

Jennifer had to respond to the friendly grins of the Lakeview Hospital staff members. The concentration required to drive Guy's unfamiliar vehicle in the heavy rain as she'd followed a crowded ambulance to the small emergency department of the rural hospital had been a challenge. Especially having to negotiate the ford across a tributary of the Matukituki river that seemed to have become considerably deeper since she and Guy had travelled the other way.

In her relief at ending the journey, she had totally forgotten how disreputable she must look. Her boots were soaked and covered in mud, as were the hems of both her coat and skirt. Her hair hadn't yet dried from her time chasing the bull in the rain either, and she knew it would be hanging like old string, looking as though it hadn't been washed for weeks.

Not that it mattered. In fact, the grin from Maggie made Jennifer feel more than welcome.

'Last time we saw you in here, you were being unloaded from the helicopter after your miracle survival.'

'And now you've come in with a miracle baby,' Hugh added.

Jennifer smiled at the baby in question, who had just passed his first thorough medical examination with flying colours and been declared fit enough to do without an incubator despite his early arrival. 'I think he's the one who made the dramatic entrance.' She glanced up to where Phil had his arm around Ellie. 'Has he got a name yet?'

'Isaac,' they both answered.

'And his middle name will be Guy,' Ellie added drowsily.

Phil grinned. 'We'd make it Jennifer, but I don't think it would go down too well at school.'

Guy was releasing the pressure on a blood-pressure cuff. He pulled the stethoscope from his ears. 'BP's up to 110 over 70,' he reported.

'Fabulous.' Hugh nodded. 'It's all looking good, folks, so I think the show's almost over. We'll get this family tucked up in the ward and make sure they all get a good rest.'

'You look like you need a rest, too, Jenna,' Maggie decided. 'Or at least a shower and a change of clothes. I could give you a lift into town in the ambulance, if you like. Where are you staying?'

'I've only just arrived,' Jennifer responded a little awkwardly. 'I haven't decided where to stay yet.'

She stared at Guy, trying to catch his eye. They needed to talk. Would he allow her back onto his own turf to do that? If he chose somewhere impersonal like a hotel, she would know that any fantasy of him being involved in the future of her and their baby was a pipe dream.

'Jenna's rental car is back at my place.' Guy didn't look at Jennifer as he spoke. 'I'll take care of her.'

The promise in those words lasted only until Jennifer had showered and changed into jeans and a comfortable pullover at Guy's cottage and shared a late lunch of soup heated on the coal range and served with crusty, thick slices of buttered bread.

The rain had stopped and sunshine was breaking through patchy cloud cover, but the warmth from the open fire was still welcome. The dogs added to the sense of homely peace by stretching luxuriously and groaning in contentment.

Jennifer's tentative contentment evaporated when Guy broke the seemingly companionable silence in which they'd eaten.

'I'll give you any support you need as far as finances and things go, but that's all I'm prepared to do.'

'I don't need your money.' Jennifer could hear that she wasn't entirely successful in keeping the sharp disappointment from her tone. 'I earn enough.'

'What did you come here for, then?'

Her tone hardened. 'I thought you'd want to know you were going to be a father. I actually thought you might want to have a meaningful place in your child's life.'

Guy snorted incredulously. 'You mean you expect me to do the decent thing and *marry* you? Is *that* what you came here for?'

Yes, Jennifer cried silently. 'No, of course not,' she said aloud.

'What, then? You think I'm going to up sticks and shift to Auckland so I see my kid every second weekend or so? You know how I feel about living in cities, Jenna. Do you really think that anything would induce me to try that again?'

'No. It didn't even occur to me to ask you to move.'

Guy shook his head. 'Don't tell me you're thinking of moving to Central and becoming a rural GP?'

'Hardly.'

Not that it seemed like a totally undesirable scenario after the excitement and satisfaction of the case they had just attended. Jennifer mirrored Guy's head shake as she tried to clear the errant thought.

'I've got a job interview tomorrow afternoon for a position of head of department.' She lifted her chin a fraction. 'It's what I've always wanted and I've worked damn hard to get there.'

'Good for you,' Guy said coldly. 'I'm sure you'll be successful.'

'I've got a very good chance. It's certainly not something I'm about to throw away.'

'And how will that work?' Guy's words dripped ice. 'Raising a child and being head of department in one of the country's busiest EDs?'

'I'll employ a nanny,' Jennifer snapped back. 'It's perfectly manageable…if not ideal.'

'"Not ideal" is an understatement.'

'At least he or she will have *one* parent available.'

'Part time,' Guy said scathingly. '*Very* part time. Why bother?'

'Excuse me?' Jennifer's jaw dropped. 'What's that supposed to mean?'

'You have your life pretty well sorted, don't you, Jenna?' Guy picked up her empty soup bowl, stacked it on top of his and stood up abruptly to carry them to the sink. 'You've escaped Hicksville and have a trendy inner-city pad. You've climbed the career ladder with admirable alacrity and now you're lined up for a top job that will leave you very little time for any kind of a family life. A child doesn't exactly fit in, does it?'

'I didn't *plan* this.' Jennifer was horrified by the succinct—and unarguable—appraisal of her life. 'I'll *make* it fit in.'

Guy turned on a tap. 'As I said, why bother?'

'Because I want this baby, that's why.'

He spun around to face her. '*Do* you?'

'Yes.' Tension was making the muscles in her jaw ache. Another part of Jennifer ached even more fiercely from the shaft of despair lodging inescapably deeper. Guy thought she was selfish and shallow enough to be unfit as a mother. And maybe she had been not so long ago, but her life had changed since then. *She* had changed. Why couldn't Guy see that? It was because it was *his* baby she was carrying that the most dramatic change of all had occurred.

'You don't need to look at me as though I'm Jack the Ripper.' Guy spoke calmly as he wiped his hands on a dishcloth. 'I'm just pointing out that you do have choices.'

'I've made my choice.' Jennifer couldn't stand this any longer. Her chair scraped on the flagstones as she stood up. 'I came here to give *you* a choice, and it's pretty obvious what that is.'

'Wait a minute! Where do you think you're going?'

'Out for a walk.' Jennifer didn't look back. 'I'll be back in an hour. If you still want to get rid of your child—and me—then you'll only have to say the word.'

'*Wait!*'

But Jennifer didn't wait, and the front door closed with a resounding thud behind her.

An hour.

It wasn't a long time when you had to choose a route from the most significant crossroads Guy had ever stumbled into. He sat by his fire, his dogs at his feet and his head in his hands.

If he said the word, Jennifer and his unborn baby would disappear from his life. He knew the level of determination…and courage, this woman was capable of.

If she chose to raise this child alone then that was exactly what she would do. What's more, she'd make a damned good job of it.

Decency would prompt her to keep in touch, of course. Guy would probably get photographs once or twice a year to mark anniversaries like birthdays or Christmas. The figure getting taller in each imaginary snapshot was frustratingly shadowy. Would it have his dark hair and eyes? Or be fair like Jennifer's? A girl or a boy?

Would he get more than photographs? Would he know when this small person smiled for the first time, took its first step or said a real word? Maybe he would receive a wobbly crayon drawing or a copy of a school report eventually.

It would never be enough. Guy thought of the way Phil and Ellie had looked holding their brand-new son and something squeezed with painful intensity in his chest. He wanted to be able to hold *his* child. To make sure it knew that he would always be there for it. To take it into the mountains and share the love he had for nature. To share some of the love bottled up inside him that had no recipient.

But…if he chose that other road, he would have more than ongoing contact with his child. He would have to have a relationship of some kind with Jennifer. The memory of how it felt to hold her swamped Guy so easily because it was so familiar, but his fantasies had never included a relationship out of the bedroom. What would she be like to live with? Even in some kind of temporary fashion—like extended visits maybe.

She'd be a challenge, that was for sure. He'd have to be very sure of his ground and prepared to fight to the death if he wanted to win any arguments. But, then, she'd also be very loyal, and if he—or the child—needed someone fighting in their corner, she'd be the perfect choice.

She was brave, too, and when he'd told her that night that she wasn't useless or soft, he'd meant it. Jennifer Allen was intelligent and focussed and probably deserved the prestigious position she was aiming for. It would take a great deal to stop her reaching a goal. For the first time Guy really registered the fact that she'd never complained once in that journey they'd made together. She had been scared, hungry, in pain and pushed to the point of physical collapse, but she had just kept going.

Guy found himself smiling. The bad weather and her smart city clothes hadn't stopped her wading around in the mud to sort out that bull today either. She was quite something, this woman. It was just such a shame that they were so far apart. Chalk and cheese. Loner and socialite. Silence and noise. City and country. Wild country at that.

Releasing a deep breath in a heartfelt sigh, Guy turned his attention back to the present. He had to decide what he was going to say because it had to be more than an hour since Jennifer had stormed out. A glance at his watch confirmed it was closer to two hours and his brow creased in a frown.

Had she stuck to the roadside for her walk or headed for the hills? Maybe she wasn't a complete townie but she didn't know this part of the country. She could have got herself lost among the ridges and valleys. She could have slipped on rocky ground, still wet from the morning's rain, and injured herself. She was pregnant, for heaven's sake. With *his* baby!

With another sigh Guy levered himself to his feet.

He'd have to go looking for her and if she wasn't on the road, there was no point in relying on the comfort of the Toyota.

'Come on, guys.' He clicked his fingers unnecessarily to alert the dogs of impending action. 'Let's take Charlie out for a run.'

Jennifer's feet hadn't been this wet and cold and uncomfortable since…since she'd trailed after Guy in their walk down the mountain. They weren't blistered again, thank goodness, but they poked out from the ends of her jeans like two big mud balls.

The despair that had propelled her to take to the hills had made her oblivious to where she'd walked, and even a small stream and ankle-deep mud hadn't done more than slow her temporarily. Whatever she'd been hoping to find was elusive until fatigue forced her to take a rest. She sat on a slab of rock near another stream and watched several tiny lizards scuttle out of the now warm late afternoon sunshine and disappear down a crack. A pair of rabbits gave her a startled glance before bounding away further uphill, and then it was just Jennifer and the vast surroundings of the Central Otago landscape.

Huge fluffy clouds scudded over the mountains, some with peaks still laden with snow. She could see the expanse of Lake Wanaka in the distance and the closer ribbon of the Matukituki river. Rocky hills flowed in every direction and obscured any sign of human existence like roads or houses.

Idly Jennifer began picking the buttercups growing beside her as she sat and absorbed the stillness and peace. *This* was what she had needed. Time out. Time to come to terms with the fact she was now bonded for ever through a child to a man who didn't want her. A man she was desperately in love with.

The persistently strong feelings she had grown accustomed to over the last few weeks had nothing to do with any post-traumatic stress syndrome or even the hormonal turbulence of pregnancy. The real reason for her apparent obsession with Guy had been blindingly obvious as soon as she'd seen him again, and the truth had become inescapable the moment she'd caught his expression when he'd watched Phil and Ellie and the baby together for the first time.

All the things she had been striving for in her life had just lost a great deal of their significance, and Jennifer felt utterly lost. Maybe she'd always been heading in the wrong direction. Ever since…

The glow of the bright petals she held distracted Jennifer. Almost mesmerised her. The last time she had picked buttercups had been to present a bouquet to her mother on one of their frequent wanders through the farm paddocks. Their special time together when the rest of the world had been forgotten and Jennifer had been the most important person in existence.

The blur of her tears made it difficult to ascertain what it was she saw appearing over the ridge of the next hill. Jennifer blinked and then stared. And then she laughed through her tears. She was still laughing and the tears had been brushed away by the time the apparition neared her rock.

'What's so funny?'

'You're a Knight,' Jennifer pointed out, 'and you've just ridden up on a white charger.'

Guy's grin lit up his sombre features. 'Charlie's hardly a charger. I was lucky to get a good canter out of him. He's just a retired farm hack but, hey! If you need rescuing then I'm your man.'

He slid off the large white horse and held out a hand. Jennifer grasped it and scrambled to her feet. The two dogs, who had hurled themselves into the stream to cool off, emerged to shake themselves vigorously and shower Jennifer with water.

'Get on behind,' Guy growled. The dogs grinned back, still panting hard.

'It doesn't matter,' Jennifer assured him. 'I'm filthy anyway. Just look at my feet!'

'Charlie won't mind. I can brush the mud off later.'

'You don't think I'm going to *ride* back, do you? I haven't even been on a pony since I was a kid, and he's *huge!*'

'You'll be as safe as houses,' Guy promised. 'Have you any idea how far you've walked? It would be nearly dark by the time you got back.' He eyed her feet. 'I'll bet they're cold and you don't want to get a new set of blisters, do you? Besides,' he added firmly, 'there's a session at the Glenfalloch pub tonight to wet young Isaac Guy Henderson's head, and you're expected to attend as the guest of honour.'

'But I haven't got anything to wear!'

Guy raised an eyebrow. 'I'm sure we can come to some arrangement. How 'bout I tell Maureen to leave the doilies in the cupboard and you can go…naked.'

'Yeah, right!'

The change in the atmosphere at the very notion of Jennifer being naked was marked. Having Guy vault onto Charlie's bare back after boosting her on board cranked it up to an electrifying level. When they started moving, with Guy holding Jennifer securely against his body, the rocking motion created a physical contact that was almost unbearably exciting.

'Do you really want to keep those?' Guy's hand touched the one of Jennifer's that wasn't gripping a handful of shaggy mane.

She looked at the wilting bunch of buttercups and smiled. 'Yes,' she said firmly. 'I do.'

When they reached flatter ground, Guy asked whether Jennifer wanted to try a faster pace. She agreed, partly because the sooner the exquisite torture of being held so closely by Guy was over the sooner she could try and get her head straight again, and partly because she felt so safe and secure in his arms that she was ready to try anything.

Charlie's steady canter felt like flying, and Jennifer laughed aloud at the sheer pleasure of it. The ride was over all too soon, however, and Guy slid down and then held up his arms to catch Jennifer as she dismounted. Suddenly she was on the ground, still in Guy's arms and grinning like an idiot. With her face upturned, she was about to find a way to express her appreciation but the look on Guy's face made any words die on her lips.

He wanted to kiss her. Jennifer's lips parted, more than ready to welcome and return the contact, but as her gaze locked with his she could see the flash of alarm and almost feel the gathering of resolve. He might *want* to kiss her—maybe even as much as she wanted him to—but he wasn't going succumb to physical desire. Whatever it was that made her unacceptable was way too powerful.

Guy turned away, dropping his hands from Jennifer's waist. 'You go ahead and get changed,' he said gruffly. 'I'll take care of Charlie.' He didn't turn his head as he led the horse away. 'It really doesn't matter what you wear,' he added wearily. 'People want to see you, not your clothes.'

There was no chance for any kind of personal conversation before heading out to the local gathering, but Jennifer was quite happy to wait for Guy's verdict. The more time they spent together, the more chance she had for more than a rank dismissal from his life.

A crowd of nearly a hundred people packed the large public bar of the Glenfalloch pub, milling around tables that groaned with the weight of the community's culinary offerings. The animated buzz of happy conversation died as Guy and Jennifer stepped through the door. Phil Henderson, a tall glass of beer in one hand, had spotted them and was tapping on his glass with a spoon to attract everyone's attention.

'Here they are!' he cried. 'Not one but two knights in shining armour. Without these two heroes I might not have my wife, let alone the most beautiful baby in the world.'

The cheer that went up, along with the handclapping, was embarrassing enough, but Jennifer wished a hole in the floor would open up and swallow her as one young man's ribald shout was heard above the general approval.

'You'd better marry her now, Doc, and turn her into a *real* Knight!'

A woman standing near the door smiled at Jennifer. 'Take no notice of Nathan, love. We've all been letting off a bit of steam, that's all. This is a celebration we've all been looking forward to.'

'I'm Lillian,' the woman introduced herself. 'This is my husband, Dave. We're the closest neighbours to the

Hendersons so I expect I'll get to see a lot of wee Isaac. Is it true he's quite OK?'

'As far as we know, he's absolutely fine,' Jennifer confirmed.

People were gathering around her and she could see that Guy was being slapped on the back and congratulated as he made his way closer to the bar. Introductions were coming at her from all directions. Hands needed shaking and all sorts of questions about Isaac's arrival had to be fielded but, to her surprise, Jennifer found herself enjoying the attention. When had she ever felt this much appreciation and respect from the relatives and friends of patients she'd treated? Mind you, she'd never had the time or inclination to spend any kind of social time with them.

A glass of sparkling wine found its way into Jennifer's hand but she abandoned it discreetly as she was edged towards the tables.

'You must be starving, dear. Grab a plate. There's plenty!'

Indeed there was. When she got close enough to the tables to see what was on them, a lump the size of a golf ball lodged itself in Jennifer's throat. It was like a time warp. These tables could have been at any country gathering in her own childhood. Steaming plates of sausage rolls and small potato-topped savouries stood by plastic bottles of tomato sauce. Asparagus rolls were doing their best to unfurl and there were even lamingtons, with cream oozing out from their coconut-drenched chocolate or strawberry coating.

Jennifer was sure she recognised two of the women she'd overheard talking in the hospital corridor the day she'd finally hauled herself out of bed. One of them eyed her with great interest.

'We certainly didn't expect to see you back in our neck of the woods.'

'I just popped back to visit Guy.'

'Hmm.' The two women exchanged a glance. 'You must have got to know each other quite well on that wee tramp in the mountains.'

'You could say that.' Guy leaned over from a conversation in a neighbouring knot of people, flashing Jennifer just the ghost of a wink. Was he also thinking of just *how* well they had got to know each other?

'And you've come back. How long will you stay this time?'

Jennifer was trying to will herself not to blush. 'Not long, but I'm sure it won't be my last visit.' Guy may have returned to his own conversation but she was sure he was listening to her words. 'This part of the country has changed my life. I think part of me belongs here now.'

Guy confirmed that he'd been listening by turning towards the women again. 'Jennifer has to get home tomorrow. She's about to become the head honcho for the emergency department in her Auckland hospital.'

'Well, it's just lucky you happened to visit today, then, isn't it?' The women nodded happily and then one drained her glass of wine.

'So you're staying with Guy, then?'

No arrangements had been made for the night, but Jennifer had no idea how long this celebration was likely to last. If it finished late, he was hardly likely to send her off looking for a hotel, was he? She hoped it would finish late and she simply smiled at the women without answering the question.

'Those savouries look delicious. Where can I find a plate?'

Maureen, the pub manager, was only too happy to replace Jennifer's missing glass when she approached the bar some time later. Guy was drinking orange juice, she'd noted, but she was hardly likely to become involved in any further critical cases tonight, was she? Just a sip or two of wine wouldn't hurt. It might even chase away the knot of misery lodged deep within Jennifer. Maureen must have noticed the direction her glance had strayed in.

'He's a wonderful man.'

'Yes, he is.' Jennifer had no argument with that.

'We're so lucky he decided to come back here to live. He could have had a high-flying career in the city, too, if he'd wanted.'

'I'm sure he could.'

'He hated the city.'

'Yes.' Jennifer wished Maureen would pour the wine a little faster, but she was dribbling it down the side of the glass, making sure the bubbles didn't escape into foam.

'He was married once, you know.'

'I did know that.' Jennifer was sure he wouldn't want it being discussed over the bar, but something in Maureen's glance made her actually lean a little closer.

'She didn't fit in,' the older woman confided. 'She was always dressed to the nines and looking down her nose at us all.'

Jennifer was suddenly very pleased she was wearing her jeans with the hems still damp from where she had sponged off the mud.

'He deserved better.' Maureen handed Jennifer her glass and smiled. 'He still does.'

Jennifer stared down at the glass in her hand. 'I don't

think he's very interested in getting involved again. Once bitten and all that.'

Maureen just smiled. 'What about you, love?' she asked softly. 'I couldn't help noticing the way you look at him. *You're* interested, aren't you?'

Jennifer simply returned the faintly knowing smile. Let them all gossip, she decided happily. She had a funny feeling that they might support her side of the situation, and that couldn't hurt, could it?

Music from a live band that included fiddlers started up and it wasn't very long before Jennifer found herself dancing. With the ancient and bearded Mack, of all people, in a fairly riotous square dance. When she apologised for her lack of expertise, his considered response of 'You'll do' made her feel ridiculously pleased with herself.

At some point much later in the evening, Jennifer was balancing a plate laden with a chocolate éclair and a raspberry slice when she found herself back in a group of local women who had clearly taken advantage of the celebratory drinks Phil had supplied.

'Such a shame Digger isn't here,' one said sadly. 'He did love a good knees-up. Especially here, in *his* pub.'

'I thought Guy's mother used to own this place.' Even the small amount of wine, in conjunction with that interchange with Maureen, had dulled quite a lot of Jennifer's aversion to gossip. Besides, they were discussing one of the few people Jennifer actually knew about in this gathering.

'It was Digger that *really* ran it.' The speaker lowered her voice to let Jennifer know she was about to receive confidential information. 'For years and years. The further Diana Knight slid into the bottle, the more he took over.'

'Lucky for Guy that he did.' Another nodded. 'That boy would have ended up in prison otherwise.'

'Or dead.'

'He was a real father to him. Only one he ever had.'

Jennifer took another sip of her wine. 'He…was fond of Guy's mother, wasn't he?'

'Worshipped the ground she walked on.' The speaker sniffed eloquently. 'He was never going to be good enough for the likes of Diana, though. She had her sights set on some flash job in the city. Finding herself a millionaire. She hated this place.'

'Why did she stay, then?' Jennifer asked.

'Had no choice really. She got herself into trouble and headed home.'

'As they do,' another woman said knowledgeably.

Do they? Jennifer wondered. With her mouth full of éclair there was no need for her to respond, but she found herself thinking about the comment as the gathering finally dispersed.

Was that what she was doing? Heading back to her roots, having got herself 'into trouble'?

'Let's go home.' Guy appeared by her side and Jennifer knew that home with Guy was exactly where she wanted to go.

It was raining again quite heavily by the time they returned to Guy's cottage.

'You'd better stay,' he told her. 'It's too late to be hunting down a motel, and this weather's getting worse.'

'Thanks.' Jennifer accepted the offer happily. She also accepted the offer of a cup of tea in front of the fire before heading off to the guest room. She relaxed on one side of the couch with the dogs at her feet. 'This is great,' she told Guy. 'And I really enjoyed tonight as well.'

'Really?' Guy sounded sceptical.

'Really.' Jennifer nodded. She curled her legs beneath her and took a deep breath. 'I'd forgotten what it was like. I have memories of evenings like that from when I was a teenager, and I thought it would be my worst nightmare to go to another one.'

'Because of the food?'

Jennifer smiled, shaking her head. 'Because of everyone knowing everyone else's business, and it coming across like they wanted to interfere. I didn't have a mother and every second woman wanted to step into that breach. I wasn't having any of it.'

'I'll bet.' Guy was smiling now but he was staring ahead into the fire rather than at Jennifer.

'They only wanted to help, though. I can see that now. They cared and I just pushed them all away. I couldn't wait to escape.' She hesitated only briefly. 'Bit like your mother, I suppose. Or your ex-wife.'

'Yeah.' Guy still wasn't making eye contact.

'I don't feel like that anymore,' Jennifer said quietly. 'I feel drawn back. I can't replace what I lost, but being here makes me realise just how much I did throw away.' She raised her gaze to where a small jar of water sat on the mantelpiece above the fire. She had put the wilted buttercups into it before they'd gone out, and now their stems had straightened and the furled petals were waiting for daylight to open again. 'And...' Jennifer added, a shade desperately, 'I want it again.'

'What?'

'That feeling of belonging. Of...of being, I don't know...important.'

'You're far more important where you are.'

'Not in the way it matters the most. I think that's why I want this baby so much. It feels more real, more important than anything else I have in my life.'

It was a long moment before Guy spoke again. 'You'll be a great mother, Jenna.'

'I hope so. I can't remember much about my own mother. I feel like I grew up without one really.'

'You and me both. Only I was missing a father as well.'

'You'd be a great father, Guy,' Jennifer said shyly.

The silence was even longer this time. 'I can't do that, Jenna,' Guy said finally. 'Don't you understand? I…I have feelings for you, and if I go there I'd end up like Digger, mooning after a woman whose standards he could never hope to meet.'

'That's not true.'

Guy ignored her. 'Or it would end up like my first marriage with the love I thought I'd found whittled away until there was only bitterness left. I can't change who I am, Jenna, and I'm not going to try. Not again.'

'I'm not asking you to.' Jennifer reached out and caught Guy's hand, the little squeeze she gave finally prompting him to meet her gaze. 'What I feel for you has nothing to do with where you live or how much money you make.' She paused and then gave her head an imperceptible shake as she tried to arrange her thoughts coherently enough to impart her message. 'Well, it does have something to do with where you live, I suppose.'

'Of course it does. We're on different planets, Jenna.'

It was Jennifer's turn to ignore Guy's comment.

'You remember when you left me by that lake? When you went off to find firewood?'

Guy nodded slowly.

'I sat there and looked at the scenery and felt the isolation and stillness of it all, and I got this incredible sense of being part of it. Being…home, I guess. I put it down to exhaustion and stress and everything, but it's happened again since then. Like today, when I sat beside that stream up on the hill, and it's even happened in the middle of Auckland when…when I've being thinking of being with you.'

Jennifer couldn't be sure, but it felt like Guy was holding *her* hand now, not just allowing his to be held.

'I've thought about it so often and I knew what it was when I saw you again today.' Jennifer's voice dropped to a whisper and the words were the most difficult she had ever had to utter. 'Being with you makes me feel like I've found everything I've ever been searching for in my life. It feels like…like I've come home.' Her need to catch a breath sounded like a gulp. 'I've a horrible feeling that I'm in love with you, Guy.'

Guy was sitting very, very still. He opened his mouth and the intensity in his eyes made Jennifer quite sure he was going to return the depth of feeling she had just expressed. Then he shook his head very slowly. Very sadly.

'It could never work, Jenna. I've been there before. I *know* it could never work.'

'You haven't been there with *me*.' Jennifer could feel fingers of despair reaching for her heart again. 'If I really want something to work, I make damned sure it does work. And we've got a good reason to try, haven't we?'

She pulled at Guy's hand, drawing it closer. Close enough to rest on her belly.

'Haven't we?' she whispered.

CHAPTER TEN

TAKING his hand off Jennifer's belly had torn a little piece from Guy's soul, and it bled far into the night.

Dawn found him walking in the hills, two bemused dogs trotting philosophically at his heels. Guy was saying nothing and it was more than clear that the exercise wasn't easing his level of stress.

He was so close to giving in. To letting his heart rule his head even though he knew it would be fatal. It was so tempting to believe her. To believe that she had found something more important in her life than her financial and professional and social success. But if he unlocked that door in his heart, he would be giving everything to Jennifer...and his child. They would become the warp and weft of his soul, and he simply couldn't allow that to happen because it would destroy him if they left.

And they would leave. Guy took a running leap to clear the small stream and kept going, a steady and punishing pace that had the dogs panting. Sure, it could work...for a while. A honeymoon period that would suck him into believing that it really was going to be forever, and that would be enough to seduce him into giving every ounce of love he was capable of giving.

Jennifer could work with him in his practice. Hugh Patterson had said more than once recently that the workload of the emergency department at Lakeview warranted extra medical staff, so he would be delighted to make use of Jennifer's expertise. Then she'd be busy with the baby, at least for a while, and her career would take a back seat.

But it wouldn't last. It could never last.

At some point she would realise what she'd given up and she would resent the fact she was stuck in an isolated community, practising skills in emergency medicine on a very part-time basis. She wouldn't be teaching anymore so she'd lose her prestigious title of professor, and having a husband and baby and a couple of dogs could never hope to fill the empty place in her life.

She'd try to hide it, of course. There'd be a gradual slide into discontent. There'd be arguments when Guy was called out and she was left to deal with some domestic crisis or chores. The kind of education available probably wouldn't be good enough for her child, and the social life would become excruciatingly dull. Guy never wanted a repeat of what it was like to be associated with someone who used their intelligence and wit to put people down, as Shannon had done so well. She'd alienated Guy as well as herself from the community and had made both their lives a misery.

Shannon had left, as Jennifer would, too, eventually. It would break his heart but it would be so much worse than it had been with Shannon because his love for Jennifer would blow any previous relationship out of the water. Even worse than that, when she left she would be taking their child with her, and that would destroy him utterly.

He would lose not only the woman he loved but a family, and he'd be exactly where he was now but with his spirit crushed beyond repair. He was better off to stay the way he was. No matter how hard it was to send Jennifer away now, it was a bid for survival. Just like that walk away from the crash site had been.

With a snap of his fingers to warn the dogs, Guy did an about-turn and headed for home. The decision was made and he would stick to it because he had no choice. And this time he was going to make damn sure that Jennifer Allen wouldn't be trailing behind him.

Despite being an early summer morning, it was cold in the empty cottage. The blackened remains of the fire in the grate offered no warmth and Jennifer had no idea how to poke up the coal range and get it started.

Guy was nowhere to be seen but she had definitely heard a door closing some time ago. Maybe he had gone out on a call. Jennifer sat at the kitchen table and zipped up her boots. She would find a cloth and wipe the last of the mud off them later. Or maybe she wouldn't bother. Exhaustion was pulling her into a space where she really didn't give a damn.

She was supposed to leave today. If she wanted to catch her 1:00 p.m. flight she would need to leave the cottage by noon at the latest. It was just after 7:00 a.m. now. Time enough to talk to Guy even if the call took some time, but could it make any difference? When he had snatched his hand from her belly last night and said it was time they both got some sleep, Jennifer had known any further attempts to throw herself at this man would just be pathetic. And soul-destroying. Something her pride should really prevent her doing.

Except…she had seen something in his eyes when she'd confessed her love for him. A reflection, or recip-rocation?

Maybe she could at least find out whether what she had glimpsed was enough to hang any hopes for a future on. Whether something might change over the coming weeks or months. If there really was no hope, then she'd be stupid not to head home and put her emotional energy into securing the position that would challenge her enough to wipe out any dissatisfaction with her surroundings and disguise the loneliness in her life. Not to mention providing financial security for herself and her child.

There was no hint of any promise on Guy's face when he strode through the door a short time later.

'You're up, then.' He nodded. 'Sleep well?'

'No. Did you?'

'Guess we could both use a coffee, then,' was Guy's only response. He busied himself getting the coal range back into action. 'What time does your plane leave?'

'One o'clock. I've got a connection from Christchurch to Auckland at 2:15.'

'What time is that interview?'

'Four-thirty.'

'Cutting things a bit fine, aren't you? Maybe you could get an earlier flight.'

'I don't want an earlier flight. We still need to talk, Guy.'

'There's nothing left to talk about.' Guy had the fridge open now, fishing out a carton of milk. 'You might like to spend the extra time with some sightseeing in Queenstown, though. You didn't get much of a chance the last time you were here.'

'I don't want to go sightseeing.' Jennifer closed her eyes but her weariness was more emotional than physical. 'We can't leave things like this, Guy. I meant what I said last night. I…I love you.' Lord, it sounded desperate and pleading in the cold light of day, but she couldn't prevent herself trying at least once more. 'You said you had feelings for me. We're having a baby. There has to be a way we could make this work.'

Guy abandoned his task, turning to face Jennifer. He shook his head. 'I'm sorry, Jenna, I really am. Yes, I do have feelings for you. Strong feelings, and that's what makes it all the more impossible. It's *because* of how I feel about you that I'm doing this. So that *neither* of us gets hurt. It just couldn't work. It doesn't matter how we feel about each other because no amount of love could put us on the same planet.'

'But I *told* you, I—' Jennifer broke off as the telephone rang and Guy raised his hand to silence her protest. She watched forlornly as he crossed the room to pick up the receiver. He thought she was the same person she had been when he'd met her. He didn't believe she had changed, and why should he? People didn't change something that fundamental. What he didn't understand was that it had been there all along for her. She had just spent most of her life trying to bury it, probably thanks to the trauma of losing her mother so young.

The realisation was still fresh. It had started while picking the buttercups yesterday, strengthened when she'd seen how they had revived in their jam jar last night and had become crystal clear during the sleepless hours that had followed. Guy had lost everyone he had loved. After the disaster his marriage must have been, who could blame him for thinking she would never last the distance? The barrier he had in place seemed impenetrable and if she kept pushing, he would just fortify his defences. She would be well advised to admit defeat, at least for the moment, and try to find a different approach.

Suddenly Guy's voice cut through the spin of emotion governing her thoughts.

'It's pretty early to be visiting. He's probably out seeing to the cattle or something first.' He listened again. 'If the ford's impassable, that'll be why he hasn't made it. Maybe the phone lines are down.'

Jennifer watched as Guy rubbed his forehead and then squeezed his temples as though in pain. 'Are they sure it's a truck? How long before someone can get in the river and check it out?'

Then he was nodding. 'I'm on my way.'

He put down the telephone pulled a mobile phone from the charger beside it. 'I have to go,' he told Jennifer. 'I have no idea what time I'll get back. Don't worry about locking the door.'

'What's happened?'

'Phil rang Ellie after he left the pub last night. He said he'd be in first thing to visit them, but he hasn't shown up and he's not answering his mobile. Ellie called Maureen to see if he'd decided to stay at the pub because of the rain last night. Maureen alerted our local cop and he's just spotted what looks like a set of tyres in the river.'

'Oh, God!' Jennifer breathed. 'That ford! It was bad enough yesterday and it was raining quite hard again last night, wasn't it?'

'Our local search-and-rescue team has been activated. I'm the medic. We're meeting at a point just down from the ford in fifteen minutes.'

'I'm coming with you.'

'You can't. This could take hours.'

'I don't care.'

'You might miss your flight.'

'I don't care.' Jennifer was pulling on her coat. 'I can get a later flight. I could ask them to postpone my interview until tomorrow.'

'I don't want you to come.'

'I don't care,' Jennifer snapped for the third time. 'This isn't about you, Guy.' She was pulling on her coat. 'You win, OK? As soon as this is over, I'll be out of your life. I'm not stupid enough to keep battering my head on a brick wall.' She was at the door now, waiting for him. 'This is about *Phil*, not *us*. I was there when his baby was born yesterday, Guy. Do you think I'm going to go home without knowing whether Isaac's father is still alive?'

Several vehicles were already positioned at the rendezvous point near where the tributary joined the larger river. The bearded Mack was there with his tow truck. Other locals had also gathered but the three men dressed in overalls and heavy boots were strangers. Guy introduced them as members of the search-and-rescue team from Queenstown.

'The police divers will be here shortly,' the team leader, Wayne, informed Guy. 'Then we'll know what we're dealing with.'

Was there any chance Phil could have survived his vehicle being swept away and overturned by the swollen river? Catching the glances of people who had shared the celebration of Phil Henderson's son's arrival last night, Jennifer thought it unlikely. And incredibly sad. Hadn't this community had enough tragedy to deal with recently?

She moved closer to a group of women who had the back of a utility vehicle covered in Thermos flasks of hot water and various containers. Maureen was using a plastic lid as a board on which she was buttering scones.

'Can I help?'

The women made space for her, and Jennifer was handed a knife and a jar of raspberry jam.

'They'll need something to eat and a hot drink,' Maureen explained. 'Especially if they have to start searching.'

'Do you think Phil might have got out of the truck, then?'

'Let's hope so.' Maureen's expression was grim as she sliced another scone in half. 'We'll find out soon enough.'

But it was nearly an hour by the time the police divers arrived and got into their wetsuits and breathing apparatus. The news had spread like wildfire and more and more locals arrived to stand vigil at the riverside. The faces were all familiar but there was no hint of the camaraderie and humour of the previous evening. These people were grim. They were all somewhere no one wanted to be, but they were there together to both offer and receive support.

It was a solid thing, this feeling of community, and Jennifer felt a curious pride at being part of it as she made a strong pot of tea and then took a plate of food to offer to the official search party. Their numbers had also grown, with police, ambulance and fire service vehicles and personnel on standby. Guy was leaning over the bonnet of a police car as he and Wayne studied a detailed map of the area.

The shout from one of the divers came just as Guy raised a mug of tea to his lips.

'Cab's empty!'

The tea slopped onto the edge of the map. 'Are you sure?'

'Affirmative. The driver's window is wound down. He must have got out.'

'Right.' Wayne was ready for action. 'We'll divide into two teams and search the banks. Maggie, you go with Pete's team and you stay with me, Guy. That way we'll have a medic on hand without having to wait for a boat to do a river crossing.'

'I'm coming, too.'

The look Jennifer received was one of astonishment. Then it became patronising as Wayne's gaze raked her from head to toe. 'I don't think so.'

'Jenna's a doctor. Specialist in emergency medicine.' It was Guy who spoke up in her support and Jennifer flashed him a grateful glance.

'She's not equipped or dressed for this,' Wayne said dismissively. 'She'd be a liability.'

'I've got a spare set of overalls in my truck.' Jennifer recognised the young man who'd made the quip about Guy having to marry her last night. Nathan. 'She can have those.'

'This isn't a Sunday walk,' another of the men from Queenstown was disparaging. 'She wouldn't even keep up.'

'Don't you believe it.' Guy pinned the man with his glare. 'Jenna could give you a run for your money any day. She made it out of the Balfour Range with me after that plane crash.'

'Oh…' Wayne's glance carried something more like respect now.

'And I, for one, would prefer to have her along,' Guy added. 'If Phil's in need of medical assistance, Jenna's the person I want to have around.'

'She saved Phil's baby yesterday.' The onlookers had been listening to the exchange and one now spoke up decisively. 'She deserves a chance to help him.'

'She should come.' Maggie sounded unusually serious, but then she flashed Jennifer an almost imperceptible wink. 'She's one of us.'

'We're wasting time,' one of the Queenstown men growled.

Wayne nodded. 'Let's move.' He turned to Guy. 'It's up to you, mate. If you want Jenna, you'll have to take responsibility for her.'

That was it in a nutshell, wasn't it?

If he wanted Jenna.

Of course he *wanted* her. He'd be mad not to. She was gorgeous, intelligent, talented and kind. She was going to be the mother of his child, for heaven's sake, but even that paled into insignificance compared to the fact that she loved *him*.

Guy watched as people fussed around Jennifer. Nathan had provided the overalls. Maureen had taken off her work boots and was now zipping up Jennifer's in their place.

'Classy,' she pronounced. 'Might keep these.'

There were encouraging smiles, hands patting her back and a lot of voices wishing her luck. Something *had* changed. There was no way that the Professor Allen from that conference would have been treated like this. Or been such an integral part of the gathering at the Glenfalloch pub last night.

He'd seen that heart to heart she'd been having with Maureen at one point when the two women had been leaning towards each other over the bar as though sharing something very private.

He'd seen her dancing with Mack, of all people, her cheeks reddened by the vigorous activity and her head thrown back in laughter at her own lack of expertise.

He'd even seen that impromptu examination of old Mrs O'Donell's bunions in a quiet corner. How could she have gone on to stuff herself with chocolate éclairs after *that?*

Maggie had been so right. She—and the others—sensed something he had refused to allow himself to believe. Deep down, where it really mattered, Jennifer *was* one of them. She wasn't—could never be—an outsider, the way Shannon had been.

Guy's mind was only half on what he was doing as they started the search down the river bank. Jennifer was a little ahead of him, keeping pace with Wayne. He hadn't seen her walking from this perspective before. She'd been trailing after him for that whole walk out of the mountains.

It seemed unbelievable now that his choice would have been to leave her behind. He actually *had* left her behind, hadn't he? For a moment the wash of shame was enough to make Guy forget that he was on a mission to try and help someone else survive.

The reason he'd tried to leave Jennifer at the crash site and go on alone had been because it had been the easy way out. And wasn't that precisely what he was doing again now? Pretending he was doing what was best for both of them when, in actual fact, he was opting out. Refusing to go with Jennifer on a journey that had the potential to lead *him* away from the wreckage this time. The wreckage of his past marriage and the rubble of other relationships he'd lost with those he'd loved.

The river was wide at this point with several channels divided by shingle banks. Some channels were shallow enough to simply walk across, but the central flow was far too deep and swift to negotiate. Huge tree branches had been swept down to clutter the banks. Some had tangled to present dams that only increased the speed of the deep water. It would be so easy for someone to have become entangled in such obstacles and then drowned. Every area needed searching, which included poking below the water surface with long branches.

'Oh...*God!*'

Adrenaline flowed at Jennifer's groan of despair.

'Have you found something?' Guy stepped over boulders and snapped small branches in the few steps it took to catch up with her.

'It's one of the presents Phil collected last night. Look!'

The sodden teddy bear had been wedged in the fork of a tree branch. Jennifer pulled it free and Guy could see the control she was exerting not to cry.

'He'll be OK after a wash,' he told her. 'We'll take him home with us.'

'It's not that...' Jennifer gulped in a breath and turned away from Guy. 'This is just all so sad,' she said brokenly. 'There's not really much hope, is there?'

'There's always hope, Jenna. Don't give up.'

But Jennifer was moving again. Guy saw her scrub the tears from her face, resolutely square her shoulders and move on, with her bowed head the only evidence of how bleak she realised this situation was and how little hope any of them had of finding Phil alive.

She was hanging in there till the bitter end, though, wasn't she?

Jennifer Allen would never take the easy way out.

She had considered staying with that plane wreckage the safer option, but she had still been prepared to follow him and risk the journey. He'd tried so hard to push her away. To cut her out of sharing any of his grief for Digger. To avoid having to care for her as well as himself. How had she felt, being left alone like that? She must have known there had been a possibility that rescue would never come. That she could have been left to die alone.

She hadn't wanted to die alone and she'd been brave enough to do something about it.

Guy didn't want to die alone either, dammit, but was he brave enough to follow her example and *do* something about it?

All it would take would be for him to summon the courage to follow Jennifer's lead this time. And maybe this was the real bid for survival in his life. Because if he was with Jennifer, he would be *really* living and not simply existing.

Jennifer was ahead of him and she wasn't looking back. Just as he had when she'd set out to follow him. But she wasn't going to be waiting on a rock for him to catch up. She'd told him he'd won. She would be out of his life as soon as this was over.

But he hadn't won, had he? He was losing here big time, and as the minutes passed, the more he could see just how much he was losing.

The teams kept in touch by portable radios. After an hour's searching they took a break. Wayne decided to split the searchers into smaller groups. Some would keep going downriver but the others would move back and search the pockets of bush and the paddocks nearby.

'He may have got himself out of the river and tried to head for home,' Wayne decided. 'I'll get the helicopter in to have a look as well.'

Another thirty minutes passed. And then another. The helicopter was hovering overhead, but they could still hear the radio Guy was carrying as it crackled to announce a call.

'Guy? Are you receiving?'

'Roger.'

'The chopper's spotted something. There's a water race at the far end of the paddock to your right where the chopper is. Can you check it out?'

'On our way.'

Guy had taken hold of her hand to help her over a post and wire fence. Maybe he didn't notice he was still gripping it tightly as they ran towards the area beneath the hovering helicopter.

Jennifer noticed. So did Wayne and the other members of their team who were following. The physical connection was broken only when they reached the ditch, skidding to a halt to peer over the long grass at the shape half in and half out of the shallow stream of water at the bottom.

'Hey!' The voice was as weak as the smile but, amazingly, the humour was still apparent. 'You're a bit slow doing the rescue bit, aren't you?'

'*Phil!*' Jennifer scrambled down the sloping side of the ditch. 'My God, you're *alive!*'

Guy was grinning from ear to ear as he turned to Wayne. 'Told you she was the best, didn't I, mate?'

Phil looked as though he wanted to laugh but groaned instead.

'What hurts?' Jennifer demanded. The fact that Phil could talk and even attempt humour was a good indication that his airway and level of consciousness weren't badly affected.

'It's my leg.' Phil groaned again. 'I got out of the river just before the truck got washed away and decided to take a short cut home. Then I fell into this damned ditch in the dark and I think I've broken my leg. Hurts like hell and I can't move.'

Jennifer didn't need to cut any clothing away to see the twist in Phil's right leg.

'Fractured femur,' Guy confirmed, having climbed down the other side of the ditch.

'You feel like a block of ice.' Jennifer let go of Phil's wrist. 'We need to get you out of here and start warming you up.'

The helicopter had landed in the paddock now and a stream of people were arriving, having heard the good news being relayed by radio. There were plenty of willing helpers to get Phil out of the ditch. Guy, Jennifer and Maggie worked together, wrapping Phil in foil sheets, putting a traction splint on his leg, giving him pain relief and IV fluids that Maggie had managed to keep warm in an insulated holder. Within a short time Phil was quite stable and relatively comfortable, ready for transport to hospital.

'Are you going to travel with him, Maggie?'

'Could do. I should stay with my ambulance, though. I am on duty.'

'There's only room for one extra.' Guy frowned as he turned to Jennifer. 'Maybe you should go,' he said quietly. 'That way you'll have time to get cleaned up and you could still make your flight. I can send your other stuff on later.'

Maggie's face fell. 'Are you leaving already? But I thought you and Guy…' Her gaze flicked from Maureen, who gave a warning headshake, back to Jennifer and Guy and she fell silent. So did all the other people who were eagerly eavesdropping.

Jennifer's throat tightened painfully. So this was it? A public farewell? Then she looked up to catch Guy's

expression and suddenly it was hard to breathe, let alone
try to swallow.

The barrier had dropped. The clouds of doubt she was
so used to seeing had vanished. What Jennifer was seeing now was a totally unguarded piece of Guy Knight's
soul. And he *wasn't* trying to push her away. He wanted
her to stay.

He wanted *her*.

'I don't *have* to catch that flight,' she said.

A candle of what could only be hope burned in the
depths of those dark eyes. 'But if you miss that interview, you might lose your chance to be head of department.'

'I guess so.' Jennifer couldn't have cared less. She
wasn't at all sure she had any interest in that job now.
The life she would be returning to would be empty and
meaningless without Guy. Shallow, even. But she had
worked her whole life towards this goal, hadn't she?

'Maybe I don't *want* to be head of department anymore.' Saying it aloud made the relinquishment of a
long-held goal seem more acceptable somehow.
Especially when Maureen was nodding so approvingly.

''Course you don't, love,' she encouraged. 'There's
more to life than just working hard.'

'You've worked so hard to get this opportunity.'
Guy's eyes were searching hers 'You wouldn't really
give it up *completely*, would you? Just like that?'

Jennifer almost smiled reassuringly, but she didn't
want to make this too easy for Guy. The harder he was
finding it, the more courage and commitment he was
revealing. It was an opportunity to find out whether Guy
felt the same way she did—that any option that didn't
keep them together for the rest of their lives simply
wasn't an option.

'I would if there was something better on offer,' she said.

'Such as?'

Maggie gave Guy's arm a shove in the short silence. '*You,* you idiot. Can't you see it's you that Jenna wants more than any job?'

Nathan hooted with glee somewhere behind Jenna. 'He is going to make her a Knight. What did I say? Man, am I *good!*'

The helicopter rotors were turning slowly now as the pilot warmed up to take off with Phil. Their patient might be quite comfortable, and appearing to enjoy the drama going on right beside his stretcher, but it was high time he was transported. A decision had to be made.

'I'll go in the chopper,' Maggie offered. 'You two can go and canoodle in the ambulance for a bit while you sort yourselves out.'

'I'm not going anywhere,' Phil declared. 'Ellie will kill me if I can't tell her how this works out.'

'A wedding's just what we need around here.' Maureen sighed happily. 'I haven't done a reception for ages.'

'Hang on!' Jennifer was horrified. However well-meaning these people were, pushing Guy Knight in a direction he was possibly only beginning to accept as an option could spell disaster. 'We're not talking *weddings,* here.'

'*I* am.' Guy contradicted her.

'Get on with it, then,' Phil groaned in frustration. 'The suspense is killing us.'

Guy caught Jennifer's hands. 'I tried to survive once without you, Jenna. I thought walking off that mountain by myself was the only way I'd make it, and I was wrong. We made it together.'

Jennifer nodded and then her lips curved softly. 'We did.'

'And…and I thought keeping my heart safe was the only way I'd make it through the rest of my life. I was wrong there, too. Very wrong.'

'You're a man,' Maureen said kindly. 'You're allowed to get it wrong sometimes.'

Mack scratched his beard. 'You'd better get it right this time, lad, hadn't you?'

Guy was apparently more successful at ignoring the helpful input than Jennifer was. She was trying not to smile again because Guy was looking so very, very serious. But then he spoke again and any inclination to smile faded.

'I can't survive without you,' Guy said simply. 'And I don't want to try. I want to share my life with you because without you it wouldn't really *be* a life.'

'Say yes,' someone shouted.

'He hasn't *done* it yet,' Phil growled. 'You have to ask her to *marry* you, mate.'

The roar of the helicopter had been steadily increasing and Guy had to raise his voice to be heard.

'I love you,' he shouted. 'Will you marry me, Jenna? Please?'

There was no need to make Guy work any harder at this. The truth was there in his eyes, and the happiness infusing Jennifer made this the most magic moment of her life…so far.

'Yes,' she shouted back. 'I love you, too, Guy.'

The cheer that went up as their lips touched was loud enough to compete with the helicopter, now more than ready to take off. The copilot was waving furiously in the background, trying to hurry up the stretcher-bearers.

'We'd better go,' Maggie yelled.

'No way.' Phil's head shake was decisive. 'They haven't finished their snog yet.'

Jennifer was laughing. She couldn't help it. It was so unromantic doing this in front of all these people, and yet it was so appropriate. There would be plenty of private time later. Time to say all the things they needed to say. A chance to touch more than their lips and to cement the promises that kiss and now Guy's hand was making as it held hers so tightly.

The copilot ran towards them. 'What's the hold-up here? You coming with us, Guy?'

'He can't,' someone shouted. 'He's busy getting engaged.'

The helmeted figure looked at Guy and then at Jenna. Then his gaze travelled down to where their hands were locked. He shook his head.

'I don't suppose she's about to let you go in a hurry, is she?'

'Not if I can help it.' Guy grinned.

'Guess we can squeeze an extra one in this time, then. Can we go now? Are you all sorted?'

Jennifer felt the grip on her hand tighten and looked up to catch a glimpse of her future in Guy's dark eyes. He was nodding.

'We're all sorted, aren't we, Jenna?'

'We've done the most important sorting,' she agreed. 'There might be a few minor details to work on.'

'How long is *that* going to take?' The copilot had already taken hold of one end of Phil's stretcher.

'Don't worry, mate.' Guy reached for the other end of the stretcher. 'We won't start now. I expect it's going to take a fair while.'

Jennifer was grinning as she followed the men towards the rear of the helicopter. It was going to take a fair while all right. She was going to make sure it took the rest of their lives.

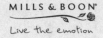

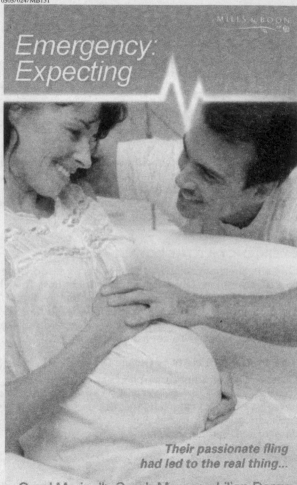

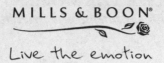

FREE

4 BOOKS AND A SURPRISE GIFT!

We would like to take this opportunity to thank you for reading this Mills & Boon® book by offering you the chance to take FOUR more specially selected titles from the Medical Romance™ series absolutely FREE! We're also making this offer to introduce you to the benefits of the Reader Service™—

- ★ **FREE home delivery**
- ★ **FREE gifts and competitions**
- ★ **FREE monthly Newsletter**
- ★ **Books available before they're in the shops**
- ★ **Exclusive Reader Service offers**

Accepting these FREE books and gift places you under no obligation to buy; you may cancel at any time, even after receiving your free shipment. Simply complete your details below and return the entire page to the address below. You don't even need a stamp!

YES! Please send me 4 free Medical Romance books and a surprise gift. I understand that unless you hear from me, I will receive 6 superb new titles every month for just £2.75 each, postage and packing free. I am under no obligation to purchase any books and may cancel my subscription at any time. The free books and gift will be mine to keep in any case.

M5ZEE

Ms/Mrs/Miss/Mr..Initials ....
BLOCK CAPITALS PLEASE

Surname ....

Address ....

....

....Postcode ....

Send this whole page to:
The Reader Service, FREEPOST CN81, Croydon, CR9 3WZ